MURDER OF A BOOKMAN

When the police are called in to investigate the brutal murder of bookseller Brian MacDonald, who's been stabbed in the back with his own letter opener, they have no trouble in finding suspects. In fact, just the opposite is true: there are way too many possibilities.

McDonald has been less than honest in his dealings, both professionally and personally. As a result, the number of individuals who loathe the man far exceed the few that held him in esteem.

But Police Detective Bentley Hollow, the chief investigator, has problems of his own: his wife has left him, and his new partner is someone he disdains. Still, he has to find a solution for the crime—and when he does, his life will be irrevocably changed! The first book in a great new mystery series.

Borgo Press Books by GARY LOVISI

Driving Hell's Highway: A Crime Novel
Gargoyle Nights: A Collection of Horror
Murder of a Bookman: A Bentley Hollow Collectibles
    Mystery Novel

MURDER OF A BOOKMAN

A BENTLEY HOLLOW COLLECTIBLES MYSTERY NOVEL

GARY LOVISI

THE BORGO PRESS

MMXI

MURDER OF A BOOKMAN

FIRST EDITION

Published by Wildside Press LLC

www.wildsidebooks.com

DEDICATION

For my wife, Lucille

.

CONTENTS

PROLOGUE

"I'm surprised to see you," Brian McDonald said cautiously, allowing the visitor to enter his home. *"You know I sell books, but it's by appointment only."*

"I remember, but I must *have that book, not just a copy or a reprint, I want the original, and I want it right away."*

"Really? Well, I'm just surprised, that's all. You know it's pricey. So you like Jim Thompson?"

"I like him—his work, I mean. But mainly I want it because it is a book that my father had in his collection years ago. It was one of his favorites. So, I want it back now."

"Well, that's nice, I'm sure. Do you have the money?'

"Of course."

"Then come in. Let's go upstairs to my office."

"You have the book here?"

"Of course. Now and on Earth *by Jim Thompson, Modern Age, 1942, the first edition in hardcover and jacket of the author's first book. 'Near Fine' in a 'Near Fine' dust jacket. A prize piece, and a cornerstone for any serious Thompson collector, or collector of noir and hard-boiled crime. So, you collect Thompson?"*

"In my own way."

McDonald shrugged, "Well, I want $25,000 for it. Do you have the cash with you?"

"Yes, but that's much too much, I'm sure you'll take a flat $20,000 cash."

"No, I don't think so. As I told you, $25,000 is my firm price."

"No, I think you will see it my way, for old time's sake. I can give you $20,000 cash right now. I have 200 one-hundred dollar bills. See?"

McDonald was silent looking at the cash being held up in front of his face. It was a big, fat pile of hundreds. Was his mouth actually watering?

"I told you, $25,000 is my firm price."

"Well, then I will walk, and you get nothing."

"Wait! Okay, okay, $20,000. You're getting a very good deal."

"Sure."

"Come into my office. You can place the money on my desk. Here is the book. Look it over. You like it?"

"Yes, and I'll take it."

"Good," McDonald replied and he pocketed the cash quickly. Then he took out a thick binder and opened it to the section beginning with 'T' and began thumbing through it. He looked up at his visitor for just a second and explained, "I just have to write the sale here in my book and take it off my list, then we will be done."

"Sure, I'll wait while you finish up."

"I'll just be a minute," Brian McDonald said, now sitting at his desk with the opened book in front of him, *his head buried in the record book busy filling in the date and terms of sale.*

His customer stood behind him watching patiently.

The bookseller's full attention was now on the wad of cash in his pocket and in looking up the sale in the book in front of him.

"There's just one more thing."

"Eh?" McDonald asked absently.

"This!"

The silver letter opener that had moments before lain innocently upon the desk was plunged full-force into the top of Brian McDonald's back. It went in deep and hard with a force and rage unexpected, down into the man's spine, scraping bone. There was remarkably little blood.

McDonald shook, froze, looked up into the face of his killer and then died instantly. His head fell down onto the desk, but the sales book was not there any longer. The murderer was holding the volume now, while the gleaming silver letter opener stuck out of the bookseller's back like a shiny beacon of death.

Next, the killer took back the cash and cleaned off McDonald's desk of all papers, throwing them to the floor carelessly, picking up a thick black marker to write an angry message in bold, fiery block letters upon the desktop.

CHAPTER ONE

"Hollow!" I heard the harsh voice of Captain Wallace bark from his corner office. "Hollow! Grant! Get in here now!"

I looked up from my desk in the squad room and straight into the face of the man sitting directly opposite me. That man was Detective Charlie Grant, a guy I hated almost as much as he hated me.

Most detective partners had desks in the squad room placed flush front to front, facing each other, so each detective would always be able to see the mug of their closest cop buddy when he looked up from his desk. Until recently, that had been my long-time partner, Don Evans. He was a great guy who had just retired, so I was now flying solo. Charlie Grant's partner, Ed Morgan, had recently died from a massive and sudden heart attack. So Grant and I were both flying solo now. We both knew that couldn't last.

Yesterday, Captain Wallace moved Grant across from me into Don's old desk. I took that as an omen of things to come. A bad omen.

Charlie Grant looked up at me, shook his head, "The old man's on a tear, we'd better get in there fast."

I shrugged, I didn't care about the old man or his problems, I had my own problems to worry about. My wife, Beth, had recently left me for a swanky doctor across town. She'd cleaned out our bank account, and she'd even taken some of the best pieces of Depression Glass that we'd collected over the years. Some of that stuff was now worth a good bit of cash. She'd taken the quality items and had left me with a quantity of second-rate stuff. I was lucky to have that left. I didn't know which was worse, loosing the wife—who had become a marginal friend and less-than-marginal lover over the last few years anyway—or loosing all that valuable collectible glassware. Being a collector myself, I figured it was a toss up.

"I'll take my time, if you don't mind," I told the guy across from me. I didn't even want to think of him as my partner yet. So far he wasn't, and I hoped that would last for a while longer. "We're not dogs that jump to our master's voice."

"*Hollow! Grant!* Get the hell in here *now!*" the old man barked out again. It was loud and full of menace.

Grant and I jumped then, right out of our seats and hurried into the Captain's small glass-enclosed office at the back of the squad room. Grant closed the door behind him softly.

Captain Tyler Wallace was an ornery old coot at the best of times who was a charter member of the KMA Club—kiss my ass—he being a few years past the retirement age where he was on schedule to get a good pension. He didn't give a damn about much and didn't care who knew it. He was seated behind his desk, which he used like a battleship to bully, intimidate and scare the hell out of rookies, and even some old coppers. This morning his face was twisted with concern and worry. "Don't sit down, gentlemen, you won't be here that long."

I looked at Grant and then back to the Captain, hoping and praying that he wasn't going to do what I thought he might do—that is, team Grant and I up on a case.

"Grant, Hollow, I'm going to team you up on this case," Wallace said slowly, allowing his words to sink in. My heart sank. I hated Grant, and he hated me. We had our reasons. "Grant, you're my best detective, and Hollow, you… I hear you collect a lot of old crap, like antiques and stuff, glass and other junk like old books. Well, don't you?

"A little," I ventured carefully. The way Captain Wallace described me, it sounded like I was the local junk man, but I only collected Depression glassware, and not much of that. Only select pieces, and at select prices that I could afford. But I was a collector and I did understand the mentality, so maybe he was right, in his own twisted, over-simplified way of thinking, to pick me for a case that involved collectors.

"Great! That's just what I need, someone who understands these freaks that collect all this old crap. Books in this case." he said, shaking his head, like it was a mystery why anyone would want to collect books of all things—much less read them!

"I'm not a book collector, Captain," I corrected him, just to set the record straight. "I don't know books at all."

"You'll learn. Doesn't matter really, you collect old stuff, so you get the idea," he looked at me sternly. Some reaction by me was called for.

I nodded.

"Good, then it's settled. We just got a call from 101 Montrose, home of Brian McDonald. The man is some kind of rare book dealer. The guy was murdered late last night, by all accounts, stabbed in the back. The body is still fresh, uniforms are there now, lab boys on the way. Get there fast and close this case."

We both nodded, got set to leave. Neither of us was happy.

"Now listen," Wallace added in a sharp but low tone, "there's something else. I just got a follow-up call from the first uniform on the scene. He found McDonald dead but he also found something scribbled on the man's desk by his body, it was some kind of message. Now keep this quiet. I don't know if it is a part of this investigation or not, but we can't ignore it. I just want you to keep it quiet."

"What's the message, Captain?" Charlie Grant asked suspiciously, he had taken out a piece of Juicy Fruit gum and was chewing away happily, like he didn't have a care in the world. If you knew Grant, that's the way he was.

"Book Collectors, Go to Hell!"

"Book Collectors…?" I stammered.

"Damn!" Grant replied, not chewing any longer.

"Get on it, guys—and you, Hollow, I want to see something from you on this—and not in the papers. Now both of you, get out!"

* * * * * *

The house at 101 Montrose was a four bedroom Tudor in an upscale part of town that oozed money and class. Grant and I walked through the yellow crime scene tape and passed the cop on duty at the front door who let us in after we flashed him our badges. "All right, Hollow, I'll take the lead on this one. We'll clear it up quicker that way," Grant said with his characteristic bravado and annoying arrogance. "I'll show you how it's done."

"Gee, thanks," I replied sarcastically. Then I couldn't resist adding, "Yeah, that's rich, you'll show me?"

He suddenly stopped walking, his gaze searching my face, "You're not going to give me any trouble on this, are you, boy?"

Boy? I guess I was 'boy' now because I was younger than he was. Or maybe not as experienced—like not experienced in taking money, doctoring evidence, framing up perps to get a case closed. That kind of experience that I knew was par for the course for cops like Grant. I remembered now all the reasons that I didn't like Charlie Grant and realized I'd have to keep an eye on him.

"Take the lead, I don't care," I said pulling back, trying to diffuse any argument, at least for the moment.

I mean, we hadn't even entered the murder house yet—and it seemed already things were getting hot between us.

"That's better," Grant told me as he walked inside the house. I shook my head as I followed him, but the blockhead just couldn't leave it all there, he couldn't resist taking another stab at my apparent weakness being intimidated by his bully words. I wasn't, but I didn't want any trouble.

It got me hot when he added, "Good to see you know your place, Hollow."

Well, that did it for me. My hand flew to his shoulder and I pulled him backwards, twisting him around so we faced each other. I pushed him hard against the wall of the narrow foyer, my face a bare inch from his own. I could see the sweat gleaming on his face now, the fear in his little pig eyes. Grant was just your garden-variety bully, after all. Maybe I was too, because no sooner had I braced him than I realized I had made a terrible mistake. It was so stupid but I couldn't stop myself. I really disliked this guy.

I'd totally lost control and barked into his face, "Listen, numbnuts, the old man says we gotta work this case together, so that means *together!* You screw around with me and I'll do you double back. Got it!"

I pushed him away from me with disgust and he lost his balance, wobbled into the wall, straightened himself, then glared at me insanely for a long tense moment. Suddenly he smiled at me. It was weird. I had to admit that his smile was even more unnerving than his usual anger and mad glare. Was I wrong about Grant? Maybe he was more dangerous than I had first though?

"You stay away from me, Hollow, you got that!" Grant barked in a low tone filled with the promise of menace to come. "You ever do that again and I'll fix you up, fix you up good!"

"You threatening me?" I said, ready to check him hard if he made a lunge at me.

I saw him pat the weapon in the holster under his arm, "Come on. Try me, just try me, asshole!"

I backed off, the situation between us was a lot worse than I ever expected and a lot worse than I needed to deal with while beginning a new case. I'd been so stupid, getting hot about his words. I knew a lot of it had been my fault, my anger at his insults, but I just couldn't keep on holding back. I knew I'd have to cool down, otherwise I'd blow the entire case. Probably my career, as well.

"Look," I told him, trying for a more conciliatory manner, "we got a murder here, so let's just solve it and get this done. Then that'll be the end of it, and of us."

"You put your hands on me, Hollow. I don't forget that."

"Fine. Look, I admit I was out of line, but you provoked me for no reason. If you want to brood about it, brood about it all you want. We still have a job to do. Now, you want to go upstairs and check out the murder scene?"

Charlie Grant looked at me hard. For a moment it

looked like he was about to blurt something out, then apparently he had thought better of it and changed his mind. He simply turned his back on me and began walking up the stairs to the murder room. I followed a few steps behind him, slowly, carefully. Expecting something. Ready for anything. This was turning out to be one big stinking morning so far.

Upstairs there were four bedrooms. It was a large house and the rooms were large. One was the master bedroom. We found out that the wife was not home—thank God! I didn't feel like dealing with some hysterical grieving widow with her dead husband still in the next room just then. We were also informed there was a maid in the house, the uniforms had her waiting in the kitchen downstairs. We'd talk to her later.

Right now we checked out the upstairs rooms. The other three bedrooms weren't bedrooms at all, I was amazed to discover that each room was ringed on all sides from floor to ceiling with wooden shelving which was loaded to the bursting point with all kinds of books. All over these rooms and even in the hallway were more shelves and more piles of books. There were stacks as tall as I was on the floor. We could hardly move.

"Damn books everywhere!" Grant muttered. "This whole house is full of stinking books."

"He's a book dealer," I reminded Grant.

"Yeah, I got it, Hollow, but, I mean, this is crazy, man."

I didn't say anything else. Grant was right for once—

talk about obsessive and compulsive collecting—and I was a collector myself so I understood some of this. Still and all, it was just too much for me to deal with. The house was large but all the shelves and piles of books made it seem so much smaller, tighter, so constricted.

"Bet there's a small fortune here, though," Grant added rhetorically, and I could see the greed wheels spinning in his crafty head. "I mean, if a guy knew just which ones out of all these damn books were worth the big money…out of all this mess…."

The son-of-a-bitch was already making pilfering plans. That was another thing I didn't like about Charlie Grant. Guys that go into people's homes—some cops, firemen and home nurses—some seem to feel they can help themselves and pick up samples of whatever goodies they like—as long as the owner is a corpse, not home, or too old and incapacitated to even know they're being robbed blind.

I sighed, "Come on, the vic is in this room here."

Grant and I entered the largest room where there was an ornate wooden desk. This must have been Brian McDonald's office. Behind the desk, in a old wooden swivel chair, sat a dead man with a knife or letter opener in his back. Brian McDonald, an older looking guy, gray hair, balding, a little overweight but it didn't look bad on him—and very dead. I looked closer and saw that the weapon was indeed a letter opener, not a knife, and that it protruded from his back, just below the neck. Nicely placed. He died instantly.

Two guys from the crime lab squeezed by us and

were taking photos, then started dusting for prints.

"We in your way?" I asked the older of the two, a guy named Ed Jenkins.

"Nah, we're almost done here. Place looks pretty clean"—then he laughed—"I mean it's a mess, but I doubt we'll pick up any prints. First thing, we dusted the handle of the letter opener and it was clean of any prints, even the vic's, so it was wiped clean before it was used. The killer wasn't a pro but he knew what he was doing. He wore gloves."

"I left the letter opener for you guys to see," Jenkins said. "We already took photos."

Grant and I nodded and took a gander at the murder wound. It was grim, the letter opener dug deep into the flesh of the upper back.

"That must have hurt," Grant offered with a wink to Ed Jenkins.

"I'll bet," Jenkins laughed with his best graveside humor.

Now that we'd seen the murder weapon undisturbed, Jenkins carefully extracted it from McDonald's back with a gloved hand and deftly placed it in a clear plastic evidence bag.

"Anything else?" I asked Jenkins.

"Well, there's the message written on the desktop. I mean, 'Book Collectors, Go to Hell!,' what the hell does that mean?

"We don't know yet," I said stumped. "Ah, Ed, keep that quite for now, okay?"

Jenkins gave me a twisted grin, "Sure. Good luck

with that! Anyway, the message was almost certainly written with one of these black sharpie markers here; we got prints off of them all, except one. I'd bet the other black markers have the prints of the victim, they were his markers after all. Wanna bet the one we found without any prints was used by the killer and was wiped clean? He knew what he was doing."

I nodded. It all meant we had nothing yet.

"What about the books? Does it look like anything was stolen?" Grant asked.

Ed Jenkins just laughed at that, "In all this mess? You kidding! Who could tell?"

I nodded, the wife might know, once we talked to her. I wondered where she was. What was keeping her from coming home? I told Grant I wanted to speak to the wife, when she came home from wherever she was, and anyone else closely associated with the victim.

"There's a Mexican maid downstairs," Ed Jenkins reminded us as he and his partner packed up to leave. "I told her to wait for you guys in the kitchen."

"Thanks, Ed, we'll have a talk with her before we leave."

Once the crime lab guys walked out, I saw them passing the guys from the morgue who were already waiting out in the hall to come in and take Brian McDonald's body away.

"Give us a few minutes, guys?"

"Yeah, take all the time you need, detectives," one of the men replied with a wry smile. "We're on the clock. *No problema.*"

I looked at Charlie Grant—my partner—damnit! I slowly closed the office door so that we were now alone with the corpse. It was quite in that room full of books, deathly quiet.

"So what do you think?"

So help me, Grant looked at me seriously and said, "The guy's dead. Murdered."

"That's a big help," I said sarcastically.

"Look, Hollow, what the hell you want? We got nothing yet. Usual suspects, boyo, that's all. See who matches up, then we get our guy," he said confidently.

"What do you make of the message written on the desk?"

"Book Collectors, Go to Hell!?"

"Yeah, that message."

"Who even knows it has anything to do with the murder?" he replied, and damn if he wasn't serious about it.

I didn't say anything for a moment, I was exasperated. I tried counting to ten before I replied. Finally I said, "Look, I suppose it is within the realm of possibility that the message had nothing to do with the murder, but I don't buy it for a second."

"So don't buy it, Hollow. What you want me to do about it. I didn't write it," Grant replied getting all arrogant on me again.

"'Book Collector's, Go to Hell!' doesn't fit in with the murder? Are you serious?" I asked incredulously.

"He wasn't a book collector."

"What?" I asked astonished now.

"He wasn't a book collector, he was a book dealer. A bookseller. Well, wasn't he?"

"Well, yes, technically you're right, but in the collecting world that's sometimes a bit of a misnomer. In any field lots of collectors deal to support their collecting habit and a lot of dealers also collect themselves."

"Whatever," was Grant's brilliant reply.

I sighed, this guy was no help, barely even cooperative. "So how do you want to go about this?"

"We talk to the maid downstairs, then the wife," he said casually.

"Fine. Then we proceed from where they lead us?" I asked.

"That's it, Hollow, standard police work," he couldn't resist jabbing me. "Maybe in ten or twenty years you'll get the hang of it."

Once we left the morgue guys came in to take away the body and Brian McDonald was gone forever.

CHAPTER TWO

The maid was seated at the kitchen table waiting for us. She was an older Hispanic woman named Felipa Calderón, Mexican, and almost certainly illegal. She was nervous, scared stiff, wanting to be any place but where she was right now talking to two detectives about her murdered boss.

"What weel happen to me?" she asked in broken English. "I need this job. I work for Mr. Brian for two years now. Good years."

"You'll be okay," I said softly. "Now just tell us about the murder."

"I know nothing," she blurted, still fearful.

"Well, what did you see?" Grant barked. "Come on, out with it or you'll be gone, on the bus back home. *Comprende?*"

"Easy on her," I told Grant.

"You gotta get their attention, Hollow, or she'll never spill. Put some fear in her and she'll tell what she saw."

I turned to the maid and told her, "Don't worry, Felipa, you won't get hurt in this, I promise you, just be truthful with us." I looked over at Grant, "Let me handle this."

"I know nothing," the maid repeated. Then at my urgings she added, "I do my work, clean the house for Mrs. Milly, his wife. I never go into the book rooms, Mr. Brian forbid me to go in there. Too cluttered. I do not know how he can work in there. So much books, piles of books, everywhere. I offered to clean it for him one day and he told me no. No. No!"

"So how did you find the body?" Grant asked suspiciously. "If you said you never went into those rooms?'

Felipa looked at Grant fearfully, "I seen him slumped over at his desk when I pass by in the hallway. I bring up towels for the bathroom. I thought Mr. Brian was sleeping, I called out to him, then *Madre de Dios,* I saw the knife sticking in his back."

"Letter opener," I corrected.

"Si, it was his letter opener. The silver one from his desk."

"And then?" I prompted.

"Then I call *la policía*," she said simply. "Will I lose my job now?"

Grant shook his head impatiently and ignored her.

I looked at Felipa, "I don't know, you'll have to talk that over with Mrs. McDonald. By the way where is Mrs. McDonald? We need to talk to her."

"I do not know," the maid snapped a bit too quickly and I could see she was lying, covering up. But what and why?

"She knows something," Grant told me glomming onto the scent like a bloodhound. To me he was just stating the obvious but I didn't comment.

"Where's Mrs. McDonald?" I asked Felipa.

"I no know nothing," she told me quickly. It was clear she was scared of saying where the wife was. Something was going on.

"We'll come back to her later," I told Grant and he nodded.

"Yeah, once we find her. We need to talk to the wife," Grant added.

I looked at Felipa and asked her, "So who do you think killed Mr. McDonald?"

The maid hardly hesitated in her response, "Oh, it was certainly Mrs. McDonald. She hated him, he was cheating on her with a Black woman. Always the Black women with Mr. Brian."

"Ah!" Charlie Grant burst out impatiently smelling another scent now, one more to his liking containing scandal and sex. This time I decided to let him run with it for just a little bit to see where it might lead us. "So Felipa, Mr. Brian liked the Black women?"

"*Sí*, before me he had a *negrita* maid, Alice Sparks, but Miss Milly caught them. So Alice was fired. She was very angry with Mr. Brian."

"Miss Milly or Miss Sparks?" I asked.

"Oh, both! Both very angry at him," she said shaking her head in disapproval.

"Well, that's two suspects," Grant said.

I shrugged, apparently so, but we'd have to check this all out a lot more deeply before we could rule anyone in, or out.

"But Mr. Brian always fighting, have many enemies,

always troubles in book business," she added. "It's a crazy, *loco* business."

"What other enemies?" I asked fishing for information. Felipa was openly talking to us now and she had apparently turned into a veritable gold mine of valuable information I hoped—or a dead-end rumor mill—or maybe both. I wanted to keep her talking, then I'd lead her back to the subject of the whereabouts of Mrs. McDonald.

"Mr. Brian have a partner, name of Spears, and they always argue, each one accuse the other of stealing. I don't know how they can be in business together. Mr. Brian's ex-wife, Sandy—such a nice lady, but sad. I met her once. I hear he treated her terrible. Then Mr. Johns of Royal Books, Mr. Brian tell me once they have a big feud that runs for twenty years! Imagine that?"

I looked at Grant, "We got enough here for three murder cases."

"Seems like that," he admitted grimly. Then Grant ran them off on his fingers one by one. "We got the wife, the ex-wife, the former Black maid he got caught *schtooking*, the crooked business partner, then the feud with his main competitor in the book business. Anyone else?"

The question had been rhetorical but Felipa shrugged, "Mr. Brian was a very complicated man."

"So it seems," I said. "Now he's dead."

"Yes," she replied as if she still did not believe it.

"Now, Felipa, where is Mrs. McDonald?" I asked sternly.

She looked up at me, "Oh, please, do not make me tell you that. It will cause much trouble. When she come home, she will tell you everything."

"Look you!" Grant barked, "tell us now or I swear I'll take you out of here!"

Felipa looked at me with pleading eyes. I looked at Charlie Grant, I knew he was bluffing, the last thing he wanted to do was bring in anyone unless it was the actual killer. He saw anything else as just one big annoyance. "Forget about her for now. The wife will turn up soon, then we'll get what we need from her."

"I don't know, Hollow," Grant said. "I don't like it."

"Come on, let's go."

CHAPTER THREE

We left the maid. She was very happy to see us go. By that time the morgue guys had already taken the body out of the house. Meanwhile, the wife still hadn't come home and it appeared she could not be found. I began to wonder why. I also began to wonder just what the maid knew and what she was covering up.

Just to be on the safe side Grant and I put out an APB on the wife, her physical description, make and model of her car. Her car was missing too. I was beginning to get a bad feeling about this case. Was the wife the killer? Or was she already dead, her body rotting away in the trunk of her car somewhere in long-term parking over at the airport?

Felipa had told us that she thought the wife was the killer—but really, was it true? Felipa had also fingered a bunch of other people as the possible killer—so what could we believe of Felipa's words? Probably nothing.

Grant and I went through McDonald's address book for info on all the people Felipa had mentioned. We decided to go and see the ex-wife first.

On the drive over, Grant and I chewed over the case.

"So what do you think?" I asked him.

"Why do you always ask me what I think, Hollow? I don't think anything," the empty-headed moron told me gruffly, he was driving and getting impatient. It was obvious he didn't even want to talk to me and that our argument of the morning still rankled. I couldn't blame him for that but we still had to be professional, we still had to work together if we were to solve this case. It was becoming increasingly difficult for me to work with Grant, and vice versa.

I decided to prod him a bit, "So you have nothing on your mind?"

"No, nothing, *nada*, zilch, you got it?" he replied sharply.

"That's just great!" I said trying to hold my temper in check.

According to Felipa, Sandy Goddard was the ex-wife of Brian McDonald. She had been his first wife. They had been married for fifteen years, then divorced three years ago and from Felipa we got the feeling the divorce had not gone very well. But as we found out, not all was as Felipa told us. Either she was outright lying; the language problem got in the way, or she only saw a small part of the total picture. Probably she did not truly know the full truth at all.

Felipa did let on to us one little bit of info that Grant found interesting. When I'd asked Felipa if she knew of any hanky-panky between Mr. Brian and his ex-wife— the type of thing a current wife might not appreciate very much—she told us, "Oh, no, Miss Sandy not like the mens any longer. She likes women's only now. I do not understand this, but she is a nice lady, she always good to me."

"Lesbo!" was all Charlie Grant had said then.

I looked at him askance but kept mum. It was a long quiet ride.

We eventually pulled up to the apartment house where Sandy Goddard lived. It was a moderate pile of brick and mortar in a less than affluent section of town. The gal seemed to be on hard times since she'd split with her husband, how hard we'd soon find out. I'd called ahead so Ms. Goddard was already waiting for us when we rang her bell.

She greeted us with a large smile, and she had the body to go along with it. She was a large women; tall and rather stately with a nice figure, a bit of an Amazon princess type with a top thatch of bright short red hair. I liked what I saw, and I could see Charlie Grant was digging her too.

I decided it was best to put away any interest I felt and get down to business right away. I told her that her ex-husband was dead.

Goddard looked shocked, disbelief and then sadness covering her face. Suddenly she blurted, "Brian, dead? Oh, no…oh my God, no!"

She burst into tears. I looked at her carefully, it didn't seem like an act. Had Felipa been wrong? I wondered about that now. It was obvious the ex-wife still had strong feelings for Brian McDonald. I also wondered if any woman would ever cry like that for me when she heard that I had died. Probably not.

Charlie Grant went and sat down next to the woman, trying to console her, putting his arms around her and then rubbing her shoulders, her neck, her waist. I began to wonder just what the hell he was doing, because it was beginning to look like he was giving her a full body message. She certainly had a full, robust body, tailor-made for it. I shook my head, realizing what had begun as a seemingly innocent gesture by Grant had become totally inappropriate, but it was his dance.

Sandy Goddard suddenly noted what Grant was doing and began to look very uncomfortable. She looked over at me.

I knew I had to step in somehow. "Grant, I think this would be a good time for you to get Ms. Goddard a glass of water. I'm sure she'd appreciate that."

My partner looked at me sharply, but then got up and went into the kitchenette.

"Ms. Goddard," I continued, quickly changing the subject from sexual harassment of a witness—or a suspect—back to normal police business, "I know this has been a big shock to you, and we are sorry for your loss. If you can, try to compose yourself, because we really need to ask you some questions."

"Yes", she stammered, making an effort to regain control.

"Your ex-husband was murdered and we need to find the killer."

She looked shocked, once more tried to dry her tears with a shirt sleeve, looked at me in evident surprise, "Murdered?"

"Yes, he was stabbed to death, sometime last evening."

"My God, poor Brian." she said between sniffles she was valiantly trying to hold back. "That's so terrible."

"Yes it is," I replied. There didn't seem to be anything else to say.

Grant came back into the living room with a glass of water and she took it gratefully, sipping slowly, "Thank you, detective."

Grant leered down at her, lusting eyes taking inventory of her body, the low-cut blouse that showed her ample breasts, though I was sure that in her grief, Ms. Goddard hardly noticed. At least I hoped so. Then Grant ruined it all when he said, "Think nothing of it, sweet thing."

Ms. Goddard looked up at Charlie Grant suspiciously then. I cleared my throat quickly to get her attention. "Ah, Ms. Goddard, can you tell us where you were yesterday evening?"

That took her attention off of my partner, thank God. Grant didn't even suspect I had saved his horndog ass from big trouble, he just leered at me, his eyes telling me to lay off and stop interfering with his play.

I looked over at Ms. Goddard, waiting.

"Well, I was...." She looked at me closely for the first time and then asked, "Am I a suspect, detective?"

"Everyone is a suspect, ma'am," I said with a wan smile. "We have to ask everyone the question. So do you have an alibi for where you were last night?"

"Of course, I was away, out of the city at a resort

upstate. I can verify it all," she told me.

"And what's the name of the guy you were with?" Grant asked. I looked at him sharply and he just grinned, like the fool he was. I waited for the other foot to drop. I didn't have long to wait.

Sandy Goddard smiled coyly, "The resort is a lesbian retreat, detective, but I am sure I can give you the names of plenty of women who saw me there all day and all evening."

I sighed, "All right, we'll get back to that." I quickly changed tack. "Can you think of anyone who would want to kill your ex-husband?"

Goddard suddenly laughed, "That's a good one! Who wouldn't want to kill Brian, might be a better question."

"Does that include you?" I asked her.

"No, Brian and I decided to go our separate ways a long time ago, even while we were married. I did not care what he did after I found out about his cheating on me that first time. Our divorce was amicable enough and he treated me rather well in the settlement," she said softly. "I'm afraid I spent my settlement too lavishly, wasted it, in fact on trips and travel, but that's hardly Brian's fault. We even stayed friends."

"Really?" Grant asked suspiciously.

"Yes, really, detective," Goddard told him boldly. "You may not understand, but some people can be adult about even the most personal things. Brian and I understood each other, we got along better after the divorce than when we had been married."

Grant just shook his head. I looked at her, trying to figure her out and coming up empty. She seemed like she was telling the truth. She also seemed to be a decent enough person, whatever that means today. Maybe she was even telling us the truth. Stranger things can happen.

"All right, then can you think of anyone else who would want to kill your ex-husband?" I repeated.

"Well, there's so many," she said, shaking her head sadly.

"Can you explain that?" Grant asked, looking at me sharply. I could see his frustration with the woman was growing, as his libido regarding her was probably shrinking.

Sandy Goddard smiled sweetly, ignored Grant and spoke directly to me, "Detective, I'd look at that bitch of a wife of his for starters. Milly. She is an evil, money-grubbing whore. Pardon my French. Brian's partner, that man Spears, I never liked him, I think he is a crook and a pervert. Then there's one of Brian's major competitors, another book seller, a big fat guy who thinks he's some tough Mafia wannabe by the way he acts. I think he could be dangerous. I never liked him."

I nodded, taking notes, asking for the names and the spellings of them along with addresses and phone numbers. She gave us what she had.

"And what about you?" Grant asked again. "You mean to tell me that there was no animosity when you and your husband split up?"

"No, it's just as I told you, we had been going our separate ways for a few years. Brian was deep into his book thing. I never understood it, but he made a lot of money doing it, he had a lot of customers. They were always looking to buy and make deals. I didn't understand it all, or care about it, really. I don't collect books. I don't collect anything. I hate clutter. So we just split and went our separate ways. Brian was generous in the divorce, he didn't argue or make trouble for me. He gave me half the assets and the old house."

"I see," I said thinking it through. She seemed truthful. "I see you're living in lower circumstances here than he was?"

"Yes, as I said, I had a financial reversal, it was silly really. I put most of my divorce money into a local business and then promptly lost it all when they went under. Brian did well in his book business though, and told me he sold a lot of big money items. We remained friends and spoke on the phone now and then. So he was able to afford the new bigger house, the new trophy bitch-wife and even an occasional mistress on the side. That was so like Brian. Oh yes detectives, he let on to me about them too, male bragging, no doubt. Brian works very hard and is doing very well for himself but he enjoys his pleasures."

"*Did* enjoy," Grant reminded her.

She did not reply, but she glared at Grant. Good, I thought, I felt like bitch-slapping his ugly mug but steeled myself to concentrate on the work at hand.

"What about his books?" I asked.

"Well," she said softly—did I see just a hint of discomfort come to her features—"I never took any interest in them. So I let him have them all in the settlement. I realize now that it was probably a mistake for me financially but I didn't care about them that much—not then—and Brian did so love his books. So as far as I was concerned he could have them all. I was just glad to be free of *him*—and *them*—and I got the house and some cash so I was happy."

Goddard sat quietly looking out the window, thinking; maybe about Brian, maybe about the passing years. She looked sad. I wondered about her. She was either the best damn actress I'd ever run across in twenty-five years of police work—and I'd run across a few, let me tell you!—or she still had genuine feelings for the dead man and her waters ran a lot deeper than I'd first thought. Brian and her, after all, had been married for fifteen years. That's a long, long time. Beth and I hadn't lasted no where near that long before she'd run off with her rich doctor, but I could see how these things went. I still missed Beth sometimes. Brian's ex-wife, Sandy, didn't seem like a bad egg, in spite of her lesbian proclivities. She was an ex-wife who still missed her ex-husband, you can't make this stuff up. It was sad, really.

There wasn't much more to ask Goddard now and it was getting late. Tomorrow is another day, as Scarlett O'Hara was so fond of saying in *Gone with the Wind*, and Grant and I had a full plate of interviews lined up for the next day's work. First among them was with

Milly, Brian's present wife, who it appears had finally turned up and was ready to talk.

Grant and I said our goodbyes to Ms. Goddard and called it a day.

CHAPTER FOUR

The next morning I met Charlie Grant in the squad room and we filled in Captain Wallace on what we had, and what we had done up to then. It wasn't much but we told him we were hoping for better success today. Then we took a ride out to the McDonald house to talk to the wife, Mildred, aka Milly.

Brian McDonald's body had been taken away the previous day and we discovered that Milly McDonald had returned home later that evening. She'd heard the news of her husband's murder on the TV news. She was in the house with her mother and sister, both of whom were there to console her. Her being the grieving widow and all and seemingly playing it for all it was worth.

We got her away from the family and put our questions to her. She was in shock, or at least that's what she told us, but she sure didn't appear all that upset. She said she had no problem talking to us.

"I'm sorry about your husband," I began, looking her over carefully. She was a petite blonde, tall and slim, nice figure, a smaller-sized version of his first wife. Brian seemed to do pretty good for himself with the ladies—his women so far were not the usual type of hefty-sized gals teamed up with most bookmen. But then, McDonald had made a lot of money his ex-wife had told us by selling high-end expensive books and various associational items to wealthy clients—so Milly was the new trophy wife. She sure looked it.

"Yes, I will miss Brian," was her only reply. She sat there looking appropriately sad I thought, but with no tears, not like the ex-wife had shown us. This woman was a cold one, for sure.

Charlie Grant looked at me hard and I could see his lips slowly spell out the word B.I.T.C.H.

I shrugged, well maybe the ex-wife had been right about the new wife, but the ex was hardly the person to give an unbiased judgment on the matter. Nevertheless, Milly McDonald seemed to me to be as cold as ice. To be sure, she looked very nice on the outside, but she seemed impatiently nasty, someone who seemed to feel royally entitled, and for the first time I began to feel sorry for Mr. Brian, as Felipa the maid called him. Brian McDonald may have made a big mistake leaving his first wife for…this…one. I just hoped the sex was worth it for the old bookman with this new, younger babe, but something told me that might be vastly over-rated too and much less frequent than he'd thought it would be.

"Yes," I responded to her words, "I'm sure that a lot of people will miss your husband. Now, can you tell us where you were yesterday and the night of the murder? We were looking for you all day. Can you tell us where you were and what you were doing?"

She shifted in the seat uncomfortably, "My alibi? Is that it? You consider me to be a suspect in my own husband's death?"

"Murder," I reminded her.

"Everyone is a suspect at this point," Grant said wearily.

"Very well, you'll find out sooner or later. I imagine that Mexican maid, Lupe or whatever her name is, probably told you all about it already."

"No," I said quickly. "Felipa told us nothing."

Oh, well, then good, I'm glad she knows her place. Anyway, you want to know where I was, I was away with Rodolfo," she said casually. A bit too casually for my taste.

"Rodolfo?" I asked.

She cleared her throat, "My pool boy. We were… what would you call it, detective…? There must be some suitably tawdry word to describe it. I'm sure you know all about such things. We were at the Holiday Inn on Route 12, all day and all night."

"Shacked up, eh?" Grant said with a lascivious leer. This was his kind of alibi and I was sure he wanted to know all the details. "I guess you can prove that?"

"Yes, if I must. I have hotel credit card receipts, the desk clerk who signed us in knows us as regulars, it will be no problem."

"And where were you the night your husband was murdered? You were not in the house and the maid was asleep," I continued.

She smiled, "With Rodolfo, of course. We have a regular thing, he is insatiable."

I nodded, but I figured she had the facts about who was insatiable reversed.

She smiled, "So now you know it all."

I sighed, "Okay, Mrs. McDonald, I'm not concerned about your and Brian's relationships, so long as they don't figure into this investigation, but I don't want anything to impede the solving of his murder."

She nodded, "Well, Brian was cheating on me too, you know. Cheating with some Black woman. I'd even caught him once, doing one of the maids in my own house. In our own bed! He was totally out of control. I think he was some kind of sex addict. You know how they can be. After that, there was no love lost between us. I was just staying here waiting for my divorce to become final so I could get half his damn books."

"Books? Grant asked curiously. "You mean you wanted half of the house and the cash? Not books?"

"No, detective. I said books and I meant books. The house is under a double mortgage and has almost no equity. Brian had little money in the bank, and less cash in hand. His true wealth was in the book collection which is what is worth the big money. All his money went into it. It is worth a million dollars, I believe. Maybe millions of dollars!"

Charlie Grant whistled loudly, "Damn!"

"Millions?" I asked incredulous. It hardly seemed possible. I looked at her closely. The greed oozed off her like sweat on a hot summer day. I figured her values for the books were way over-inflated, much like the spouses of too many collectors who always think the collection they have inherited is priceless. It may well be priceless, but not in the way they think it is—which only means cold cash to them. I figured McDonald's books may not be worth anywhere near what his wife thought they were worth.

"Probably a million dollars, who can tell. I'd have to look them up, each and every one of them," she explained. Then with a smile she added, "I was to get half of them in the settlement, now that he's dead, it looks like I get them all."

I looked at Grant and he allowed a brief shiver—she was one cold cookie.

"But there's something I don't understand. With so many thousands of books here—I mean this house is loaded to the rafters with them—how can you tell which books are worth money and how much each one is worth?" I asked.

"Oh. Brian had his Value Book. It is a thick binder he kept up to date religiously. In it he wrote data on every single book he had that was worth big money. There are thousands of them. Do you know how many of them are valued in the five figures? Anyway, he also listed in there what he paid for each book, where he got it, and what each one is worth in the present market. He kept up with sales and auction results from all the major houses. Everything is in that book."

"So where is this Value Book?" I asked.

Mrs. McDonald shrugged, "Gone? Missing? Lost?

Who knows? When I heard what happened last night I ran upstairs to Brian's office...."

"Were he was murdered?" Grant added sharply.

"Yes," she replied hardly missing a beat, not even looking at him, or me. "I went up to get it. It was gone. Brian always kept it laying in the center of the top of his desk."

"Right where someone wrote that message." I said softly.

She nodded, "Brian was a very neat man. Orderly. Everything had a place and was always kept in its place. Now I discovered that everything usually on his desk was thrown to the floor and someone had written that crazy statement about book collectors. Brian wasn't even a book collector," she said sharply.

Grant looked at me with a 'I told you so' look.

"'Book Collectors, Go to Hell!'" I reminded her.

"Yes, can you believe it?" She laughed, then added, "Well, if you knew Brian, and some of those book collector people he dealt with, that statement may actually be accurate. They're an odd bunch. Brian certainly was."

"So what does that message mean to you?" I asked her.

She looked at me blankly, "I really have no idea."

"So this Value Book is still missing?" I continued.

"Yes, it's strange, it's nowhere to be found in his office. Brian never let it out of his sight, it never left that room. I think it may have been stolen."

"By the murderer?" Grant asked, I could see he was

egging her on.

Milly McDonald shrugged, "I guess so. I certainly don't have it and it's not anywhere in this house—and believe me—I've looked! That's my meal ticket."

How nice, I thought. I was going to ask her if she'd killed her husband, but then remembered she'd told us about her alibi—which we'd check out soon enough. But something just told me that her alibi was good, it wasn't even worth looking at her for this. If she'd done it, Brian would have disappeared, never to be seen or heard from again. No, this had to be the handiwork of someone else. Maybe his partner or an upset client?

Grant and I were both back at square one but we did know one thing—that Value Book was important, it was missing, and the killer probably took it!

"We find that Value Book," I told Grant on the way out to our car, "and we find our killer."

"I'd like to get my hands on that book too," Grant said grimly but somehow I didn't think his reasons were the same as my own.

* * * * * * *

Next on our list of persons of interest, as they say, was Brian's partner in McDonald & Spears Rare Books, Alex Spears. However, before we left the McDonald house, we had a chance to speak with Rodolfo, the pool boy. He was a good-looking young man, tailor-made for the gigolo role. He corroborated the wife's story in every detail. He even showed us photos! They were very provocative.

"Mrs. McDonald knows about these?" I asked Rodolfo.

"Of course, it was her idea," the pool boy responded with a wide grin.

Grant looked them over carefully, then put some in his pocket claiming he needed them for evidence. I didn't want to think about it.

"So the wife and the pool boy?" Grant said later as I drove us over to Alex Spears's address. He was McDonald's partner. Grant ran though his notes and added, "So we got this Brian McDonald and the former maid—Ayesha Sledge—and the new mistress—Alice Sparks. Then we've got the bitchy current wife and the lesbo ex-wife. Quite the messy life our Brian lead. What is it with these book collectors, Hollow?"

I shrugged, like I could answer his question. I could see Grant was stymied. This case was beginning to give me a headache too. I was wondering how it would eventually settle out. Would we ever find out who the killer was? And why murder Brian McDonald? Was it really for his damn books? That was just too weird to believe, even for book collectors, I thought.

And where was that Value Book now? That surely had to be the key to it all.

We met Brian McDonald's partner, Alex Spears at his home on the other side of town. It was another large house but not so luxurious as the one we'd just left. There was no pool, no pool boy, and no maid; only a big empty house—except for the books—the place was full to the brim with books. Books all over the damn place! Shelved, stacked in piles on the floor, some of the piles as tall as I was.

And cats. Cats everywhere and into everything!

We'd called ahead and Spears let us in and escorted us inside carefully to his office, another room like all the other rooms in the house with shelves that ran from floor to ceiling stuffed tightly with books. I walked among the stacks gingerly, fearful of causing some type of book tsunami. There were all kinds of books, everywhere, all over. Most of them were wrapped in some kind of clear plastic covering, or in clear plastic bags. It was worse than McDonald's place. We were surrounded and could hardly move.

Then there were the cats. If I thought the book clutter was bad, the cats made it worse. They were everywhere too, sitting on the tops of piles of books and looking at us like we were enemy interlopers, or chasing each other between the stacks, meowing and clawing at each other. Sometimes they knocked down stacks of books to the floor with a resounding crash.

"I hate when they do that," Spears told us as he got up to rearrange the stacks or put a fallen book back in its proper place on a shelf or atop some pile.

The smell of cat piss was the worst part of it all. I mean the odor was overwhelming, pungent and sharp. It was bad. The cats seemed to have free run of the place. I wondered if there was some unwritten law about books and cats existing in some symbiotic relationship. I knew Grant hated cats, so that made it more bearable for me to be there. I was actually enjoying his discomfit.

"Terrible news about Brian," Alex Spears told us once we were seated as comfortably as possible, in his tightly cramped office. He was smoking a pipe and the rich cherry flavor thankfully covered up some of the strong feline odor in the room that threatened to overcome us at any moment. I could see that Grant was none too happy and wanted to get out of there as soon as possible. I couldn't blame him, but we needed to have a good long talk with Spears first.

I looked around me, taking in the full impact of the room. It was actually rather large, but seemed so small with all the shelves. I only learned later that all of them were double shelves, where the books were placed on them in two or even three rows. The piles of books all around us made me feel like a western pioneer in a covered wagon surrounded by attacking Indians. We were surrounded and we could hardly move at all. The effect was very claustrophobic. The cat smell was getting to me too now. I wanted out as soon as I could and Grant just held his nose and cursed under his breath.

"We need to ask you a few questions, Mr. Spears," I began.

He nodded affably, "Ask away. Sorry about all my little friends here. I just can't resist cats and kittens, and they all go along so well with my books."

"How many of these cats you got here?" Grant asked in amazement.

"Oh, my cats? Probably twenty, but some keep dying

on me and then others get born, so it fluctuates."

I grinned with joy when I saw Grant frantically pick up a big fat tabby cat that had suddenly clawed his way up his leg to flop upon his lap like he owned my partner, and Grant quickly threw it to the ground in angry disdain.

"That's my Mr. Poe," Spears said with a smile full of pride.

"Mr. Poe?" Grant growled, quickly brushing cat hair off his suit.

"Yes, Mr. Edgar Allan Poe. All my cats are named after famous authors," Spears said proudly. "Mr. Poe is really very friendly, loves to be petted, not at all like that damn Hemingway, he is just trouble, trouble, trouble! Watch out for him, I warn you."

I looked around suspiciously, imagining Hemingway laying somewhere unseen ready to spring at me in ambush.

"Yes," Spears continued, "they really are an active bunch. Mary Shelley had a litter of three, H. P. Lovecraft, Dashiell Hammett, and Raymond Chandler. John Steinbeck or Ian Fleming impregnated both Agatha Christie and Louisa May Alcott, begetting C. S. Forrester, Victor Hugo, Mickey Spillane and Robert E. Howard. Howard recently died, he was much too young, just like in real life."

I looked at Spears incredulous as he continued.

"Charles Dickens is really a very nice fellow, for a cat, a true gentleman and A. C. Doyle and his brother—he's the only cat I allow not named after an author—Sherlock Holmes—are a friendly pair. Emily Dickinson begot John Dickson Carr, Max Brand, and Geoffrey Chaucer. The oldest cat I have is Old Homer, I've had him for nearly twelve years. I think that sums them up," Spears finished.

"How nice," Grant replied sarcastically. "You know, you're a very sick man. Do you know that?"

I saw that Spears looked hurt and I couldn't but help feel sorry for the old guy. It was obvious all he had in the world were his books and his cats. I wondered if the cats peed all over the books but though I looked, I didn't see evidence of that. They were probably all fixed but the cat boxes on the floors of every room made the smell pretty bad. I decided to change the subject to focus more on the reason we were there in the first place, hoping to get away from cats and the cat smell.

"What about the books, Mr. Spears?" I continued looking around me in awe. He was an older man, small sized, and as I looked at him I could foresee the day, when he, or one of his cats, would run into a stack of books that would knock over all the other stacks. Then he might end up being buried alive under hundreds of pounds of books. Death by books! I shook my head, that was weird; the claustrophobic atmosphere and breathing all that strong cat box stink must have got to me a lot more than I realized. I was amazed that it didn't seem to bother him at all.

"Oh, the books, now that's different. I have exactly 35,145 hard covers, 505 bed-sheet magazines, 3,500 slick magazines, 250 vintage newspapers, 2,000 various digest-size magazines, 1,850 pulp magazines, forty-five boxes of various manuscripts and ephemera, and some 95,000 paperback books of all sizes and formats—give or take a dozen." he said proudly.

"You counted them all?" Grant asked incredulous, shaking his head in disbelief.

"I keep very precise sales records, sir." Spears shot back sharply but I couldn't tell by his tone if he was proud or insulted by what Grant had asked him. "Accurate records are the heart and soul of success in the book business."

I nodded, it made sense. I was a Depression glassware collector myself so I understood the collecting mentality. It could get a bit kooky sometimes, but these book people, they seemed to extend the term "odd" into undiscovered realms of weirdness.

I saw Grant idly pick up a book that was laying on Spears desk, he hefted it in his hand as though trying to guess it's weight like some carnival barker. It certainly looked like some old, poor condition relic, almost falling apart in Grant's hands. If Spears was selling junk like this, he sure couldn't be making any money in the book business.

"Be careful with that! Put it down now!" Spears shouted at Grant, suddenly very angry. "My God, be careful, that's so delicate you can damage it easily. Then I'll have to mark it down from 'Good' to only 'Fair'."

Grant dropped the book back on the desk, "This old thing?"

Spears fumed, made an effort to calm himself, then picked up the book and held it carefully in his hands, away from us and out of our reach. Then he said with exaggerated feeling, "This old *thing*, is a thing of beauty, a rare and lovely volume, it is *A Pearl of Great Price* by Joseph Smith."

"Yeah? So what?" Grant said with a shrug.

"So what!" Spears actually growled at us. "So what! You, young man, are a dolt!"

"Easy, Mr. Spears, maybe you can explain to us the significance of this book?" I asked, hoping Grant was too inundated by claustrophobia and cat smell to do anything to the old man at being called a name. I allowed a thin smile, maybe Grant didn't even know the word "dolt" was an insult? I watched Grant cover his nose and mouth with his handkerchief as he mumbled menacingly.

Spears nodded, all of a sudden serious, "Yes, all right. This book is very rare, it is the third book written by Joseph Smith, the founder of the Church of Jesus Christ of Latter Day Saints."

"The Mormons?" I asked, trying to show him that I knew something about something.

"Correct," Spears said quickly, now taking the role of school teacher to us dunderheaded students. "This particular book is a rare British edition from 1851, originally it was published in wraps, that essentially means it is an early paperback. Even allowing its present worn condition, it is conservatively estimated to be worth from $30,000 to $50,000."

Grant looked at the old man, then at the old book in his hands with eyes bulging. "You're shitting me?"

"No, Smith's first book, was *The Book of Mormon* which founded the religion, and is even more rare, of course."

"Of course," I said.

Spears looked at me sharply, "But this edition is quite unique, being the first British reprint of his third book about Mormonism."

I gulped thoughtfully and looked over at Grant.

"All that dough for just one book?" Grant stammered in wonder, looking back at me in disbelief.

"For one book?" I repeated, suddenly realizing that there might be a lot more to this rare book business than I had ever expected. The collector in me was really paying attention now. This was nothing like the glassware field, at least not the field I knew about. This was big money, the type of money people killed for! And big profits, at least it looked that way to me. I might have to take a serious look at what opportunities there were in this collecting area. Maybe I'd speak to Spears about it in more depth after this case was over.

Alex Spears took the book and carefully placed it in a clear plastic bag and then put it high up on a shelf, away from us, no doubt. "I just got it today from a dealer in England who had no idea what he had. Lucky me, but not every day is Christmas in this business, let me tell you. There's a lot of lean times between the rare flush times. I was just taking the book out of the Fed Ex box when you rang my doorbell. I didn't even have time to bag it yet."

"Yeah, what a damn shame you didn't get a chance to bag it," Grant added sarcastically.

I ignored Grant. "Mr. Spears can you tell us about Brian McDonald and your business together?"

"Sure," Spears replied lightly, now that his precious book was safe from us barbarians. When you got right down to it, he seemed like an odd but agreeable sort, friendly in his own way, willing to talk. I just hoped that he would have some good stuff to tell us. He began it by telling us, "Brian and I were in the rare book business for 30 years, so long ago. We were partners since college days. In fact, Brian put himself through college by buying and selling books. He was that good. After a few years we began to make some nice money dealing in high-end first editions, manuscripts and letters, even hyper moderns. As you can see we each keep our own stock in our own homes, selling by appointment only. It's worked out better for us that way. Brian's death is a tragic loss to the field, but it was not entirely unexpected."

My ears perked up at that. "How so?"

"Yeah?" Grant blurted, scenting something other than cat piss for the first time since we'd entered the house. "Now let's get to the nitty-gritty."

"Well, I mean, it was the life he lead. I mean, for a bookman, Brian was all over the place; wife, ex-wife, mistress, even doing the maid and then getting caught doing it. What a mess! He told me all about it of course," Spears said with a rather lascivious leer. "He liked the Black women but always married White. Strange really, most bookmen I know prefer Asian women. Oh well, regardless, it must be confusing being so sexually promiscuous and having to keep so many stories straight with so many different women. He was always like that, even in his college days, and it got him into no end of trouble. I remember one irate husband that swore to kill him…."

"Husbands too?" Grant mumbled in exaggerated awe.

"Oh, yes, but that was many years ago, detective."

"Mr. Spears let's concentrate on the here and now. Who do you think would want Brian McDonald dead?" I asked simply.

"Oh, well…almost everyone. We all hated him. Even me. He could be such a *putz*. He was cheating me in the business, you know. We were supposed to split the profits on every book we sold equally, after expenses. He never did. Oh, he'd send me a check now and then for a few hundred dollars, but that was just to keep me quiet. But I knew he was selling in the tens of thousands of dollars, steadily on a weekly basis, sir."

"Really?" Grant blurted curiously. "The guy was pulling in that much moolah?"

I looked at Spears, "Is there really that much money to be made in bookselling?"

Spears laughed, "Certainly not only in rare books, any kind of books, sir, if you have the right ones. Most bookmen I know are collectors, they only sell books because they love books. It's that simple. They love the book business, that means they love matching the right book with the right reader or collector. They use the money they make to buy more books! Brian was different, he was all about money—and of course sex and women. But he did have a gift. It was like he instinctively knew the best price he could get for any book and then match it to the perfect buyer. Sometimes the only buyer! It was like magic. The key was, he knew collector's and had the contacts, and of course, he had the books people wanted. I don't know how he got them, or where he got them, but he had them, that's for sure. Brian was a crook and a con man, a weasel and a cheat, but one hell of a bookman."

"So who do you think killed him?" Grant asked impatiently, all this book talk was bugging him.

"You mean aside form me?" Spears asked with a wink and a nod. The guy was playing with us now and I could see that it was getting Grant pissed off—which I kinda liked.

"Yeah," I said, "aside from you."

"Well, I mean, isn't it obvious…?" he told us with obvious simplicity.

By then Grant had had enough of him and his books. I saw he was still covering his nose form the cat stink, then he shouted, "No, it is not obvious! Now are you going to talk sense or do I take you downtown!"

"Downtown? Booked for murder?" Spears almost smiled, and damn if he didn't look positively excited by the prospect. "Why, that would certainly be interesting. I've never been 'downtown' before. Never!

News of it would be sure to help my business—some good notorious publicity—I'm sure it would improve my sales of crime fiction and true crime. I specialize in those fields, detective."

I sighed, this was getting us nowhere. I began to wonder if the guy was crazy, or just crazy like a fox. "So look, all kidding aside. Do you have any idea who would want Brian dead?"

Alex Spears nodded, "Aside from almost everyone who knew him, or anyone he ever ran across, detective, sure, I can tell you who did it if you want."

"Yes!" Grant shouted full of anger. "That's what we want! Spill it!"

Spears looked at my partner carefully, a bit leery at his impatient outburst. "It has to be his wife, Milly. Yes, certainly. Brian even mentioned it to me a couple of weeks ago. He said she wanted to divorce him and take all his books."

"Is that right?" I asked.

"Yes, imagine that? She wanted to take *all* his books. I mean, if I had a wife and she was going to take *all* my books, I'd have to kill her too. I surely would. She would leave me no choice." Spears said seriously, and damn if it didn't look like he meant every word of what he'd just told us. Then he added with a smile, "I mean, if someone is going to take *all* of a man's books—what else is there for a man to do?"

"You're right about that," a sarcastic Grant blurted angry now, annoyed and ready to get the hell out of there.

I shook my head, "Thank you, Mr. Spears," then I got up to leave. I'd had enough myself, and the cat smell had finally gotten to me, to the point where I was actually dizzy.

"But," Spears added quickly, mysteriously, "it could have been his chief competitor, Andy Johns. Johns stole one of his high-end clients and was moving in on Brian's territory. It could very well have been Johns. Those two were always at each others throats."

I just nodded, Grant looked at Spears like he wanted to strangle him. At that point, I wasn't even sure I'd interfere if Grant decided to act upon that impulse.

"Then of course, there is Alfred Smith, a real whale in the book world, high-end collector, spends a lot of money. He complained that Brian ripped him off on a big six-figure edition just last month. He said the book was woefully misrepresented. He swore he'd get his money back or take it out of Brian's hide. Smith's always been a pain in the ass to us dealers, but he pays big money for big books so everyone tolerates him. He's a bit of a late payer though."

"Do you know if Brian got paid for that six-figure book?" I asked Spears.

"I'm sure he did. Brian would never give up any book before he was fully paid. He would make sure he got his money before he ever gave Smith the book."

"What was the book?"

"I don't know. Brian, like most book dealers liked to keep that information mum, especially during—and soon after—the initial stages of a sale."

"Do you know anything about Brian's Value Book? I heard he kept a binder of all his valuable items with information on them in it," I asked.

"No, not really, but I assume he kept such a book, many dealers—and even some collectors—do so. It helps if you keep accurate, precise records on all your holdings."

CHAPTER FIVE

We left Alex Spears and headed out across town to the man who was said to be their chief competitor in the bookselling business, Andy Johns of Regal Books. In the car along the way Grant and I talked about what we'd just heard from Spears. I was actually surprised my new partner was so talkative but I guess the case was bugging him as much it was me and he needed someone to sound off on about it.

"That guy, Spears, is a nut, Hollow," Grant said simply. "A freakin' nut!"

"Maybe."

"No maybes about it! All those books, all them lousy cats, that damn smell. I thought I was gonna puke a dozen times. You know what? I think he did it. I think he murdered his partner."

"Why do you say that? Not to get the books. He wouldn't get them. He had to know that. The books would go to McDonald's wife, Milly." I said casually, but then I wondered about it. "Wouldn't they?"

"Would they?" Grant asked suspiciously.

That got me thinking and I thought about it for a while. Was there some sort of deal in the partnership?

Maybe a secret will, or legal document, some contract that said Spears got all of McDonald's books upon his death? Maybe even vice versa? Could that be?

Probably not, I thought, but then again….

"So the partner is my chief suspect," Grant stated as if he had finally solved everything—like the genius he was. "Or maybe the wife? Maybe both?"

I shook my head in desperation, "I don't know."

"You don't know, Hollow! What the hell! What are you talking about?" Grant barked annoyed that I was not onboard with his brilliant theory.

"She was divorcing Brian, so she had a motive, I agree. She would have gotten half of the books—or the equivalent value in cash, anyway. So why kill him?"

"Greedy bitch, Hollow! Simple as that," Grant said all-knowingly. "Half wasn't good enough for her, she wanted it all."

I nodded, "That's possible, but I wonder if there is some contract regarding the books in the partnership."

"I never thought of that, Hollow," he said, looking at me, still with disdain. "I thought that old coot was hiding something. So maybe he is our boy after all?"

I didn't say anything about that. It was way too early for one thing, but mostly I didn't see Spears as a killer. Not the type at all. I liked the wife much more than the partner for the murder—but she had an air-tight alibi. I decided to shelve all these thoughts for the moment and any further talk with Grant until we arrived at our next destination.

* * * * * * *

Andy Johns of Regal Books turned out to be a large fellow, actually quite obese, bald head, bad skin and a ruddy but smiling face. He smiled at us even when we told him we were cops. That surprised me and it got Grant suspicious right off.

Johns, unlike most of these book dealers, had an actual physical book store. In that regard, he seemed to be a rapidly diminishing breed, because from what I'd learned from Spears, independent book stores would soon be a thing of the past. Like the dinosaurs. As well as the very idiosyncratic and independently-minded people who owned those stores. It was quite sad really, an important and even charming part of our culture was melting away to be lost forever.

Andy Johns lived in the small orderly apartment above his store. I assumed he owned the building which was probably the only way he could afford to remain in business. He took us on a tour through the store, lined with rows of shelves of books. It was a well-ordered used book store that he told us also specialized in rare first editions that he proudly pointed to in a special group of glass display cases behind the front desk where the cash register was located. He was proud of his store, one of the last of the independents in our city, and talked about its rich history since he'd founded it in 1974 when he was right out of college.

Johns lead us to a stairway in the back, then upstairs, huffing and puffing all the way up each step. I feared he was going to have a heart attack right there at any moment and he was sweating profusely, even though it was far from warm. Once inside his apartment, I was surprised to see that there were very few books, only a couple of shelves in one common room. The rest of the place was a neat and orderly as Spears was messy. And not one cat was in evidence. Thank you, God!

"Those there," he said, pointing to the only shelf with books upon it that I could see in the entire apartment, "they're all sold. My online sales, the main part of my business these days. I have to package them up for mailing."

Johns walked us into a small living room and over to some very comfortable-looking chairs. We sat down and got right down to it.

"So, what do you guys want?" Johns asked us, dropping himself slow-motion-like into a deep recliner with a heavy breath.

"You heard about Brian McDonald?" I began, looking for his reaction.

"Yeah, murdered they said on the TV news. I won't say I'm sorry, that bastard stole some of my best clients from me."

"The way were heard it, *you* stole *his* best clients," Grant countered sharply.

"Hah! So you been talking to Spears. That old guy is a total liar, you can't believe a damn word he says," Johns replied hotly.

Charlie Grant and I looked at each other, I saw my detective partner roll his eyes in exasperation. I actually felt his pain. Almost.

"So who do you think killed Brian McDonald?" I

asked Johns.

He laughed, "It could be anyone."

"Even you?" I asked bluntly.

He smiled but just shook his head no.

"So then, where were you when Brian was killed?" I asked.

"Oh no, it was not me." Johns added quickly now that he thought he was becoming the focus of our efforts. "I mean, it could be me. I hated the guy enough to do it, I guess—but no, I didn't kill Brian."

"I suppose you have an alibi for the time of the murder?"

"I suppose I do," he replied defiantly.

Grant and I were quiet for a moment. Waiting.

"Well, we'd really like to hear it, Mr. Johns," I prompted.

"The night of the murder I had a book signing here. Two local authors and their fans, we launched their new books. *The Crossbow Murders*, the new one by Betty Flavory, latest in her Archery Murders series. Very hot! People getting killed with bows and arrows—a very modern setting. Great fun! Then I had Simon Kent here, he came out with a rather thin but sensationalized and unauthorized biography of that new pop star—Lady…what's her name? Anyway, the store was full of people and we had a nice wine and cheese book event all evening."

"And you were here all evening and that can be verified?" I asked.

"Absolutely," he replied simply. "Where else would

I go?"

I looked at him, that could be checked out easily enough later. "So do you have any idea who killed Brian McDonald?"

"Well, my bet is on that crazy bastard, Alfred Smith. I mean, he was really hot to get his money back from Brian, from all I heard about it," Johns told us almost *sotto voce*, like he was letting on to us some magical top secret in the book world. "I sell to Smith too, he buys a lot of high-end pricey books. I hear he had some huge inheritance. He's a real octopus."

"Octopus?" I asked curious. I'd never heard the term.

"Yeah, octopus, like in he's got eight hands and he uses them to make sure he gets to have everything. Got his hands in everywhere and on everything. A completist. But unlike everyone else, he's got the cash to actually be a true completist. Anyway, I heard that Brian screwed him on a big deal, almost half a million bucks."

"For one freakin' book!" Grant blurted, he was shaking his head now. With what he'd heard about the value of that old Mormon book from Spears; now with this, Grant must have been thinking he was in the wrong profession.

So was I, I had to admit.

I let a wry grin play over my lips, knowing the collector field from my glass collecting, I knew it was not always that simple. Big dealer scores of high-value items with corresponding big money sales were not common. Most often, the item—whether book or glassware—will sit on a shelf unsold for months, if not years. The dealer ends up just tying up a lot of needed cash in an item that does not sell. Or he'd have to sell it at a loss to recoup his outlay. That would eat away any potential profit. It happened all the time. However, that rare big sale that came along from time to time really made up for it. It made it all worthwhile.

Johns looked over at Grant, "Yes, from what I heard, it was some illuminated manuscript, something like that, something really rare. I think Brian stole it from some university library somewhere. You know, there's a lot of that sort of thing going on these days. It's all on the QT, of course. Or at least, a lot more of it is happening than people realize. I remember there was some guy in the Midwest, a really big case in the news a decade or so ago. He stole out of university libraries all the time. Thousands of books! Really valuable stuff. When the F.B.I. raided his home they found it stuffed to the rafters with books, boxes of rare letters, manuscripts and more—almost all of it stolen. I think that's what Brian was into. That's the only way he could get the kind of rare, high-end, quality material to replenish his stock and be able to sell on such a regular basis."

I looked from Johns to Grant, "That puts an entirely different spin on this murder, if that's true."

Grant shook his head, things were getting too complicated for him and he didn't like it.

I continued, "If what you just told us is true about his stealing, how can we prove that? Where would he get the books from? I assume he wasn't doing the burglaries himself?"

Andy Johns shrugged, "I'm an honest dealer and I run a legit store here. I sell books because I love books. You understand? I actually read them. I collect the ones I read, re-read the good ones. I also love turning readers onto new books that I have read and liked. It's a personal thing. From time to time I have people bring in a book or collection they want to sell to me and I know it *could* be stolen. I mean, I look at the item, then the sort of person who wants to sell it to me, and sometimes it just don't add up. You know? So it could be stolen. Or it could just be some kid selling grandpa's old books. Totally legit. That happens too. Who can really tell. I'm not in the FBI, I don't verify every buy. I do the best I can. Sometimes I buy it, sometimes not. I've rarely had anyone bring in the kind of high-end items Brian specialized in. I'm not hooked into selling to that high-end library and museum market, except for a few other customers I've cultivated over the years, which Brian has taken away from me now."

"I see," I said, afraid I was not really seeing anything at all. I was wondering where we were going to find out about those stolen books. If this new branch of the case turned out to be true, it might give us a totally different reason for Brian McDonald's murder—and a totally different perp.

"I'm not hooked into the crooked end of the market, either," Johns added sternly, showing his distaste. "Maybe Al Spears would know, if you can get him to talk. Maybe Alfred Smith, the collector, would know. I'm sure his collector mania is sufficiently out of control to overcome any scruples he might have once had about buying stolen books. To me, and most honest dealers and collectors, such theft is not only a crime, it's blasphemy. Blasphemy against books and the entire field."

"Blasphemy?" Grant asked with a grin.

"Yep, that's how a lot of us feel," Johns said seriously, his eyes sharply looking at Grant. "Of course, that wouldn't play with a guy like Brian McDonald though, and I'm sure Spears and Smith are the same way. Well, maybe not Spears. I'm not crazy about him, but I guess he is honest. I do have to admit it. We just don't get along—mostly Brian's fault—him being Brian's partner for so long. Hell, Maybe Brian, Spears and Smith were in this all together? Like some secret conspiracy?"

"A book conspiracy?" I asked mildly curious.

"Yes, that's it, a damn conspiracy!" Johns replied almost dreamily. "A real biblio-murder conspiracy!"

Grant just shook his head, muttered under his breath, "They're all freakin' nuts!"

"Thanks for your time, Mr. Johns," I said, then Grant and I got out of there fast.

* * * * * * *

"So what's next on the list?" Grant asked me once we were in the car and set to drive away from Andy Johns store.

"We have to talk to that collector, Alfred Smith, then

maybe Brian's mistress, Alice Sparks—and maybe even that former maid, the one he had a dalliance with, Angela Sledge," I told him.

"Just three more to go, and we're still no closer to closing this murder," Grant said impatiently. "You know what I think? I like the partner for this. Thing is, we have to check to find out who gets the books after Brian's death—the wife, or the partner?"

"Then let's go back and see Spears about that," I said, hoping we'd get down to the bottom of that question. I also wanted to find out what Spears knew about Brian's theft of books from university libraries. There seemed something much deeper there that needed to be brought out to the light of day.

Grant shrugged, having no better idea, "All right, let's do that."

CHAPTER SIX

Al Spears was not happy to see us again and his face showed it, but our faces showed him that we were not happy with his bullshit story of a few hours earlier. That had told us nothing and sent us on our way knowing less than when we'd first gotten there.

"Murder's a serious charge, Mr. Spears," I told him flatly, laying it out. "Your story doesn't add up. Care to explain it?"

"Explain what?" he stammered, growing concerned now.

"You told us Andy Johns stole Brian's best clients—Johns told us Brian stole his clients. Now which is it?"

Spears laughed mildly, the tension melting off his face. "Oh, that's all you wanted to know? Look, detectives, everyone steals clients and contacts from each other in this business. We all buy and sell, and then resell, to each other all the time. This field is more incestuous than a hillbilly whorehouse."

Grant shook his head in annoyance. I could see that he didn't buy Spears explanation, but I was a collector and I knew collectors. What he said seemed valid to me. However, I had something else on my mind that

I wanted to put to Spears but Grant spoke up before I could get it out.

"What about that Value Book?" Grant asked sharply, looking at Spears intently, daring him to lie. "You knew about that?"

"I never saw it, but I assume Brian had some type of book to keep records. We all do. I mean, we all have something; a book, a printout or a database on a computer, something to keep records of our stock and prices. Brian didn't use a computer, so he didn't even have a printout, so he had to have some kind of hand-written record book, but like I say, I never saw it," he said simply.

I nodded, that seemed to fit. Even Grant seemed to acknowledge what Spears said, though reluctantly.

Now to the real reason we'd come back here to see Spears. I said, "Tell us, who gets McDonald's books now? He's dead, so who inherits them? You, or the widow?"

Spears looked mildly surprised by my question, "Why, the widow, she gets them all, of course. What would ever make you think otherwise?"

"Are you sure?" Grant asked acidly, suspicious as ever. "Maybe you and McDonald had some kind of secret business agreement or hidden contract, some letter of understanding? Maybe there is something in his will? Tell me now. We will check this out, Spears, and if you're lying to us...."

"Being honest with us now," I added, "will go a long way to keeping you off the suspect list. It's a list you do not want to be on, let me tell you. You can't sell books from prison."

Spears looked at me seriously. Shocked. He brushed away Edgar Allan Poe. The cat meowed and ran out of the room as if highly insulted.

"They won't even let you have any books in prison. Well, maybe one or two paperbacks, but not a fine collection like this—and no cats either," I added, sealing the deal.

Spears gulped nervously at that last remark, which really seemed to get his attention. "No, I'm telling you, Milly gets it all, I am sure. That's why Brian and I had our books separate in our homes, instead of in one central location. That way no wife, no family, would get all our stock in the event of a death or the break-up of our business."

"We'll check that, Spears, so you better be telling us the truth," Grant growled, giving the man a touch of his bad-cop routine, though he seemed mollified for now. He was probably already figuring another angle on the murder and making the wife for the killer.

"Detective, I am telling you the truth. I swear."

I looked over at Spears: he was relaxing, he was calming down.

Now I was ready to get to the real reason for *my* visit and why *I* wanted to talk to him again.

"Where did Brian get all those quality, high-end books he sold for such big money?" I asked Spears.

"I don't know. I assume he bought them on the market, like we all do. From other collectors, estate sales. Also probably from the Internet," he said simply, but I could see he was uncomfortable talking about this and it was obvious he was hiding something.

"Really? You and Brian weren't involved in any crooked dealings, selling stolen high-end books, maybe stolen from college or university libraries?" I asked more forcefully.

I could see Spears become uncomfortable, growing nervous.

"He's holding back," Grant said with a snarl. He could smell deception, even through the cat odor that permeated the house.

"Mr. Hollow…."

"Detective Hollow," I corrected sharply.

"Detective Hollow," Spears said nervously, careful now. "Do not link me with anything Brian may have done. Please. I did not know Brian's intimate business, just some snippets of what he told me; the usual woman trouble with his wife, things like that, some rumors in the trade about other dealers or collectors. But you are right, he did seem to come across an unusual amount of quality books and ephemera that he sold for big money. It was really quite amazing. I have to admit I was jealous about his sources. They were good. Almost too good."

"He ever tell you where he got any of these books?" I continued.

"No, and that in and of itself doesn't mean much. All dealers guard their sources and contacts most jealously. They do not divulge them, especially not to another dealer. A competitor. Sources and contacts are the lifeblood of our business and of our success."

I nodded, being a collector myself, I knew what Spears was saying was true. The collectible glass-ware field, especially with Depression Glass was very competitive and sources and contacts were guarded like gold.

"Okay, I'll buy that now—up to a point," I prompted, because I could see there was something on Spear's mind. Something just wasn't sitting well with him. "I see you're holding back. What is it?"

"I don't know, Detective Hollow," Spears said carefully, "I don't know. There's something that I always wondered about regarding Brian's business. Brian came across some incredible items—truly amazing—books and ephemera that are hardly ever seen on the open market these days. It was not anything that would draw attention from the news media, he wasn't selling the *Madrid Codex* or Guttenberg *Bibles* wholesale, nothing like that, just items that you saw once every ten or twenty years. And there was just too much of it. I mean, it was like he had a secret vault somewhere or a time machine where he was able to get the stuff, or maybe he was buying it…on the Black Market."

"A Black Market in books?" Grant asked surprised. He gave me a look like now he'd heard it all.

"A Black Market in *rare* books, yes…and in famous author letters, manuscripts, and other valuable ephemera, most definitely." Spears explained simply. "Then there are illuminated manuscripts, rare Dark

Age volumes hand copied by Irish monks in the twelfth century, papyrus scrolls—not the Dead Sea Scrolls, mind, but almost as old—ancient Roman and Greek texts…. You get it? Anyway, Brian seemed to find it all and sold it all. I believe his biggest buyers were not the type of collectors I and most of my brethren sell to at all. Brian sold to large institutional collections, mostly university and college libraries, museums and the like. Some rich foreign collectors, too."

I looked at Spears and smiled, asking incredulously, "Are you telling me that the same institutions and libraries Brian sold to—were the same ones he was stealing from?"

Spears gulped nervously, grinned sheepishly, "I never thought of it that way. I don't really know. It could be possible. Many of these large institutions have no idea of their holdings—other than the one or two privileged authors or popular collections they hold close and dear. Everything else is usually stored in cardboard boxes piled off in some corner of some basement building never even having been opened and examined since it was first given to the library. No one knows. No one cares. I hesitate to say this, but in some cases Brian might have even been doing the world a favor by making this material available to collectors again—to those who truly cherish these items. Rather than have them lay in a box in a room for years, or decades, in some cold, moldy basement, slowly being damaged by insects—or worse, destroyed by a fire or flood and lost to us forever. It happens, detectives, it happens all too often. I'm not approving of this, like I say, but I understand it. Regardless, I have no real evidence of just what Brian was up to, only a gut feeling that I did not want to think about. It is as simple as this. Something was not right in the way Brian was selling books."

I digested all this before I spoke, looked over at Grant, who just looked bored. Well, there'd be no help from him.

"Would Brian's lost Value Book have all this data in it? Including where he got the book originally and the cost?" I asked Spears.

"It may, it should, it could. Like I say, I've never seen this book, but perhaps," Spears replied.

I looked at Grant and he shrugged, "Coulda, woulda, shoulda...," was all he said.

"Am I a suspect, detective?" Spears asked me cautiously. Gone now was the frivolity of hours before exhibited by him upon our first visit. Now at the thought of being charged with his partner's murder Spears was seriously concerned. Even afraid.

I wasn't buying Spears as our killer, but I knew Grant had a hard-on for the fellow. Then there was also the wife. I guess Grant was putting two and two together and coming up with five, or seven, or whatever as usual, and figuring out which one of them would fit best to close the case. He never asked me nor cared what I thought, he just wanted the case closed so it would all go away.

"If you were being charged, Spears, we'd cuff you

and bring your ass in right now," Grant said with a twisted grimace. "What we want is information on the killer."

"I want to know about how and where McDonald got those books. Who was he partnered with?" I asked Spears, who looked at me with alarm since he was McDonald's partner and thought he would somehow be implicated in something nefarious. "I mean, who was he partnered with in these book thefts? Who was stealing the books for him?"

Spears though about that for a moment and eventually shook his head in consternation. "There's not many book people—dealers or collectors—who would ever consider such a thing. In the book world, it's looked upon as...a kind of...."

"Blasphemy?" I supplied the term Spears had been looking for, which I remembered Andy Johns using with us earlier.

"Yes, correct...it is book blasphemy...it is blasphemy against books, against knowledge, which is what we all prize most," Spears said dead serious now.

Grant laughed at that, insultingly nasty.

Spears just sighed, adding, "I admit there is the odd crook here and there when it comes to stretching the rules of selling, or taking advantage of a client, but out and out burglary? And of a library?"—he said the word 'library' like it was absolutely sacred.—"No, detective, I know of no one, nor could I think of anyone, who would ever do such a thing."

"Yeah, well, what about that collector freak, Alfred

Smith, that we heard about?" Grant asked quickly. "He seems like a greedy fuck?"

Spears gave us a mild laugh, "Alfred is a dear friend, but a murderer? Never! However, you are right about him being a greedy fuck, he's greedy for books, or at least greedy for the books he wants. But he would never do anything to put his collection in jeopardy, or do anything that might separate him from it. Like something that could get him jail time. You have to understand him, like I do. He loves his books—better than he does people. Yes, he would buy a stolen item—no one ever asks any questions about that, and I'm sure he has some stolen items in his collection—either known or unknown. But would he go into a university library, pretend to be doing specialized research, sign in under his own ID—or even worse, a fake ID—to access a special collection with the thought of theft? Never. Would he kill Brian McDonald? Impossible!"

I sighed, Grant just hit his fist upon the table. I knew he felt like his best bet had just busted out. I looked at Grant and he had a blank look on his face. This was getting to him. Well, screw him, I thought.

"I've had enough of books and book people," Grant growled finally, ending his sentence with a curse, which could have been at Spears, or me, or books in general. I figured it was at me, because he was looking at me when he said it. "So what now, Hollow?"

I shrugged. What now, indeed.

I looked back to Spears. "Look, if Brian was stealing rare books and other stuff from university libraries and special collections, it would have to be through someone who knew rare books. Someone who knew what to look for, what to take, right?"

"Of course," he said simply, but then he explained, "Your average criminal, any B&E guy, even a top cat burglar—remember I specialize in selling crime fiction and true crime—would never even consider mere 'books.' They want money, or gold coins or jewelry, stuff they can turn into cash right away. Certainly not books! No, if Brian was stealing books for resale, he was doing it all by himself. Remember, these are prized books in special collections, locked cases, locked rooms even, and you have to sign-in to view them and handle them. You must show identification and have legitimate credentials as a scholar, journalist or collector doing serious research."

I nodded, Spears had a point. It wasn't any conspiracy or gang of book thieves. Brian McDonald was doing the thefts all by himself and it should be easy enough to find out for sure how he did it. On our way out I told Spears to make a list of places for us to contact. I told him I'd call him first thing tomorrow morning for the list.

* * * * * * *

When we left Spears' residence I told Charlie Grant my plan. He wasn't happy about it. It would mean a lot of phone work tomorrow morning, which he hated, but he admitted he didn't have any better ideas and that it might yield some results.

"Look, today's shot. Early tomorrow I'll call Spears and get that list from him of ten local libraries that have the kind of stuff McDonald was selling. Then we'll check their records to see if McDonald had ever signed-in to access any of their collections. Then we'll have him!"

Grant looked at me with a scrunched up face. "Look, Hollow, I'll go along with this but I can't see how it gets us any closer to finding McDonald's murderer. So he was stealing rare books? So what?"

"Maybe someone found out about it?" I proposed, trying to whet his interest.

Grant just looked at me and laughed. He laughed at me and maybe he was right. It was a long shot. It wasn't like Brian McDonald had a partner doing the stealing with him—or for him. And I didn't buy the notion that Spears was involved. Even Grant seemed to have dropped that idea now and seemed to be concentrating on the wife, Milly.

"So where does that leave us?" I asked him.

"In the shit," Grant shot back quickly.

I nodded. "I'll see you in the squad room tomorrow morning."

"Whatever."

CHAPTER SEVEN

The next day was the third day after Brian McDonald's murder and I was no closer to finding his murderer than I had been when Captain Wallace had first paired me up with Charlie Grant. That had proved to be a cop partnership created in hell, but I knew I'd have to make the best of it. Worse than that even, I had to make it work, and that meant finding the killer and closing the case. Otherwise I was sure Captain Wallace would take any failure out of my own hide.

When I walked into the squad room that morning I saw Grant was already in with Captain Wallace. The office door was closed and they were talking rather animatedly. I could imagine what the topic was, and it wasn't the McDonald murder—or perhaps only peripherally. I walked over to the end of the room and when they noticed me approaching the office Grant opened the door and walked out. He came straight over to me.

"I just wanted to tell you, Hollow," Grant stated with maximum sarcasm dripping from his voice, "I asked Cap to take me off this damn case. You've made a mess of it. I told him because of you, it will go cold case by the end of the week. He didn't like that. Now you've got us looking for stolen books? I asked him to split us up as partners. I told him you're a freakin' nut case and that I want out."

We were quiet for a long moment after that, just glaring at each other.

Then I realized something, Grant hadn't lowered the boom. I smiled, told him with a snicker, "So I guess we're still partners and you're still on the case."

Grant's face grew beet red and he strode away from me almost apoplectic. When he was a few feet away I heard him shout, "Asshole!"

"Moron!" I barked back loudly.

"Fucking asshole!" Grant screamed out as loud as he could. The entire squad room looked at him and then over to me. Some of the guys laughed. Others clapped. They loved good cop-type entertainment.

I sighed, what the hell could I say to top that? Call him a 'double-fucking-asshole'?

I went over to my desk and sat down, tried to calm myself and then placed a call to Al Spears. He was up and waiting for my call, ready with the list and he gave it to me over the phone. I quickly wrote it down. He'd been thorough, not only giving me the names of ten local university libraries and special collections that were excellent prospects, but he also included the name of a contact person at each location and their phone number.

"Thanks, Mr. Spears," I said, surprised by his length of cooperation, "this is a big help."

"No problem, you'd be amazed what you can do on

Google and the Internet. Good luck, and let me know how it all turns out."

I thanked him again, then hung up the phone. I cut the list in half and then called over Charlie Grant.

"What the hell you want now, Hollow?"

I gave him his half of Spears list. "Here, make the calls on these five. I'll call the other five."

"So what are we looking for?" he grumbled.

"We want to know if Brian McDonald signed-in to get access to any of these special collections."

"I know that, idiot! I mean, so what does it mean if we find anything? Why are we doing this?"

I looked at Charlie Grant hard, the bastard was really trying my patience. I didn't want to reach over my desk and bitch slap him into a stupor—I mean, actually I did—but I'd have to cool it with that type of thinking for now. Instead I told him, "Just do it, then we'll go on from there."

"Whatever."

We made the calls.

It took a lot longer than either of us ever thought it would. Going through college and university bureau-cracy, even in the library field, turned out to be just unbelievable. I called and spoke to a bunch of overly academic guys and gals, all anal retentive types, dourly officious and ultimately annoying to the point of making me want to scream at their blockheaded-ness. Over-educated idiots. I mean, did these people take stupid pills? Finally I was able to get them to clue into the fact that I was investigating a murder and asked about the sign-in sheets and Brian McDonald's name. They gave me endless rigmarole about privacy considerations and rules so I had to take them through the entire process, then go through their supervisors. I got the feeling none of them really liked cops at all. When any info was able to be pried from their cold bureaucratic academician fingers, I came up empty for a lead. That left me dead in the water.

I reluctantly walked around my desk to where Charlie Grant sat at his desk making calls, "Anything on your five with McDonald?"

"No. Nothing," he said flatly. "They never heard of him."

"Really?"

"Yeah, none of them ever heard of any Brian McDonald. His name is not on any of their sign-in sheets."

That just didn't ring true. I looked at Grant and he looked back at me with a wicked told-you-so sneer, happy my little plan had sunk faster than the *Titanic*.

"What now, genius?"

What now, indeed.

I stood there a moment thinking, or trying to think. Finally I said, "Look, Brian McDonald was definitely going into these libraries to steal stuff, just like that ex-Clinton official Sandy Berger. Remember him? He was convicted of stealing a lot of top-secret presidential documents from the National Archives, all stashed in his pants and socks."

"Yeah, Sandy *Burglar*. I remember him."

"Anyway, if someone could do it with presidential papers at the National Archives in Washington D.C., it wouldn't be much of a stretch for Brian McDonald to do it at some understaffed libraries here in the city," I offered.

"So?" was Grant's only reply.

I looked at him closely, he was being no help at all. I could see he didn't give a damn about helping me or working the case—he wanted off it in the worse way. I knew I'd have to play this almost all on my own. So be it. No sweat really, maybe it was better that way.

"Look, I'm going to call my five names again, get their fax number and send them that photo of McDonald we got from his wife. Then we'll see if anyone remembers him. You call back your five and do the same thing, okay?"

"All right, Hollow, I'll try that. One more time, then that's it. Maybe he used an alias or an assumed name."

"He used something," I said.

Then we got to work, made the calls again, explained everything all over again, then faxed over the photo to the contacts Spears had given us at the ten libraries.

Then we waited.

An hour later I got the first call back from the Wilson University Library. Director Harold Crowhank whined into my ear, "Yes, I recognize the photo, detective. He has been here on numerous occasions but not under the name you gave us, not under Brian McDonald. Oh no, not under that name at all. We have no listing for him under Brian McDonald."

"Then what name do you have him listed under?" I asked sharply, impatient now and chomping at the bit for a break. I knew this might be the break we were looking for.

"I'll have to ask the staff," Crowhank said thoughtfully, "you see, they do most of the grunt work here."

"Don't they check IDs?" I chided.

"Of course they do, but you have to understand these are, for the most part, pimple-faced freshmen trying to earn a few bucks at a scud work job. Or simply volunteers. They don't run the library or investigate IDs. They look at a driver's license, see if the photo matches the person with the ID, then take down the name. They're not the FBI, they can't tell if an ID is fake or not, and we don't want them to do that. We don't want to inconvenience our visitors, many of whom are influential people in the media or scholars doing important research."

"I see," I said softy. "No wonder so much stuff is being stolen."

Crowhank picked up on that at once, I could feel the tension in his voice, "Stolen? Are you telling me the library has been the victim of a theft in one of its rare papers collections?"

"Nothing we can prove yet, sir, so calm down, please," I said. "Just talk to your staff and get back to me as soon as you can about the name that goes with that photo."

"I will do that right away," Crowhank said, then hung up.

I checked with Charlie Grant next. He was having some trouble, waiting for people to get back to him who were slow in responding. It set him off.

It was near noon, Grant was getting antsy and got up from his desk and just walked away towards the large double doors at the end of the squad room.

"Hey?" I shouted. "Where you going?"

"If you must know, I'm going to lunch," he said coldly.

"You could let me know," I told him.

"I don't have to clear anything with you, Hollow, remember that," he said sharply, then he walked out of the squad room in a huff.

I fell back into my chair with a groan, staring at the phone, willing it to ring, but it was as dead as my chances of any promotion in this department. Some of the guys had ordered in and I had them get me a hero, then I got a coke from the machine in the hallway. It was a quiet meal, I sat alone at my desk, trying to figure this case out and coming up empty.

Then the phone on my desk started ringing. The phone on Grant's desk also started ringing.

I picked up my phone right away, it was Crowhank, "Detective, Hollow?"

"Yes, sir," I said trying to keep calm, hoping this might be the break I needed.

"Detective Hollow, we had a match. One of our second year students put the face to a name."

"Not Brian McDonald?" I asked hopefully.

"Oh no, not at all. Get this, he told me the name used

was Alex Spears," Crowhank said proudly, like he was enjoying being my own personal junior G-Man.

Alex Spears? I shook my head, either Spears had been playing us all along—which I could not believe— or Brian McDonald was a lot more cunning than I'd given him credit for. This didn't look good. Spears could be a dead end.

I looked up as I saw Charlie Grant come over to his desk and pick up his ringing phone. He started talking to the caller. I tried to hear what was being said, wondering if it was some news we needed.

"Detective?" Crowhank asked, getting my attention back to his call. "Are you still there?"

"Oh…yes, of course, Mr. Crowhank, I'm right here. Just thinking."

"Well, I hope this has been of help to you. Are you sure there has been no theft in my library?" he asked, which I realized was his main and only concern now.

"Honestly, we don't know yet."

"That sounds bad," he said, his voice tense, nervous.

"I won't sugar-coat it for you. We're looking into things but we just started. This is just a sidebar on a murder investigation. I'll let you know if anything comes of it," I told him. I wanted to get off the phone and see what Grant had come up with—if anything.

"A sidebar? The Wilson Library is not just a sidebar, detective, even in a murder case. It's an important institution of higher learning to our city, to our nation, a repository of some of the most priceless collections of letters and papers written by major authors, scientists and politicians—the movers and shakers of our nation for the last one hundred years!"

I sighed, he was certainly correct, but I had nothing to tell him now and I wanted to cut the call. "As soon as I find out anything, Mr. Crowhank, I'll let you know."

The other end of the phone went silent for a moment, then Crowhank said, "I'll hold you to that, Detective," then he hung up.

I shook my head in exasperation, put Crowhank and his problems out of my mind and concentrated on Brian McDonald. So McDonald had been using the name of his partner Alex Spears? He had a fake ID, probably a driver's license with Spears' name on it but with his own photo, something that looked good enough to get past some college kid with the attention span of a gnat. So, was McDonald just using the fake ID, or was he planning on framing Spears if the thefts were ever discovered? I thought about that and realized it was most likely both. McDonald was a cunning bastard. No wonder he had been murdered.

I got out of my chair and walked around my desk towards Grant. He was off the phone now and I told him what Crowhank had told me.

"Yeah, what I just heard jibes with that, Hollow. The guy at Cornell Library Special Collections, told me the photo definitely matched a man who kept coming in to examine certain author collections. The name was Alex Spears."

I nodded, "But it wasn't Spears, it was McDonald."

"Yeah, so Spears is in the clear, I guess," Grant

admitted reluctantly. "This Brian McDonald was a sharpie all right, using his partner's name like that, but I can see the smarts behind it. Every time I get a room with a hooker I sign in under the name Bentley Hollow," he laughed wickedly.

"Nice one," I said, wondering if he was telling me the truth.

"So now what? I mean, knowing McDonald stole rare books for resale tells us he was a crook and a weasel, but it doesn't get us one inch closer to his killer," Grant stated.

I had to admit it, my square head partner had a point there.

I had another plan I'd been formulating while I'd been on the phone, so I told it to Grant now.

"Listen, I think it's time we split up. Why don't you go back and speak to the wife about the books and see who gets them now that McDonald's dead. It should be her. If you have time left, maybe run by the ex-maid—McDonald was caught doing her by the wife—then maybe pay the mistress a visit? She might know something."

Grant smiled, I knew he'd jump at the female bait I was putting out there to get him out of my hair. "Yeah, okay, I been curious about all these women all along—see if they're as hot as McDonald thought."

I shrugged, "Whatever."

"What about you, Hollow?" he asked suspicion suddenly clouding his face.

"I'm going back to talk with Spears again, see if I can

find out why McDonald used his name to sign-in and what his reaction is to that. I don't think he's the killer but he may know more than he is letting on. I also want to see if he ever did research himself at any of the ten libraries he gave us. He seemed to have a lot of information on them, like he'd been there before. Makes me wonder. Then I'm going to talk to that ex-wife again."

"The lesbo?" Grant laughed, giving me a throat-cutting gesture.

"Yeah."

"Well, you won't get nothing from her, I tried. If I couldn't melt her you won't have a ghost of a chance. She probably hates men. They all do."

I wondered why. "Thanks for your concern."

"Just trying to set you straight, Hollow. Get it? Straight? You're barking up the wrong tree."

"I'm not barking up any tree, Grant, she's a witness, that's all."

"Yeah, sure," he laughed. "I'll see you back here tomorrow morning."

"Tomorrow morning," I said as I walked away.

I couldn't get away from Charlie Grant soon enough. Now I was on my own, Grant was doing his thing and I was doing my own thing, and that's the way I liked it. It was good to not have to look at his beady little eyes and see that smart-aleck look on his face.

CHAPTER EIGHT

I didn't think we'd get much from Grant's visit with any of the three women he had agreed to talk to. I just wanted him to do something he thought might be useful—or better yet, just fun—anything that got him out of my hair. The wife, Milly McDonald was a pretty straight-ahead greedy bitch looking for a large cash payday on her husband's left behind books—their cash value, that is. The two other women McDonald had had affairs with—the maid and the mistress—I didn't expect much from them either. Then again, you never knew. I wanted to remain hopeful. I'd just have to wait and see what Grant dug up, if anything. Meanwhile, I'd go my own way, and that's the way I liked it.

I spent the rest of the morning with Brian McDonald's partner, Alex Spears, at his home, talking about Brian, books, and the ins and outs of the book business—in between the cats. The cat smell hadn't abated since I'd been there last. I tried to put all that out of my mind as I concentrated on business.

"Back again," Spears said carefully as he greeted me at the door to his house. "You're not here to arrest me, are you?"

I laughed, "No, Mr. Spears. First off, I want to thank you for the library leads you gave me."

"No problem, Detective Hollow," he said. "Did they pan out for you?"

"Yes, actually, they did."

He smiled, a bit excited that he was able to help the cops in a real murder investigation. He was a crime fiction reader and true crime buff and it was coming through now in his reaction to my news. "Well then, by all means come in. You must tell me all about it."

So I told him all about it and it didn't make him happy at all. In fact, he was in an uproar of righteous indignation, and then sudden worry. "My God! My good name will be ruined, my business ruined! How could Brian do such a thing?"

"McDonald didn't want to use his own name to sign-in, that would prove he had been to each of these libraries—and who knows how many more?" I offered.

"Oh, my, it's even worse that I thought then. Brian traveled extensively. He may have been doing these thefts all across the country. I am most distressed to hear this news, Detective Hollow. He used my good name, my own good name!" Spears was absolutely beside himself with trepidation and I tried to calm him and get him to focus on talking about McDonald and the book business. It took me a while. I had to impress upon him there would be no liability or criminal charges against him because McDonald had used his name fraudulently.

"You're the victim here," I told Spears. "What

happened to you was essentially identity theft. You can not be held accountable for what Brian did."

Spears sighed, breathing deeply, obviously much relieved but still quite concerned. "That bastard! That son-of-a-bitch! He not only stole from our business, he stole rare library books and he stole my identity! I tell you, Detective Hollow, with what I know now, if Brian McDonald wasn't already dead, I'd kill him myself!"

I wasn't shocked by his words.

Spears looked at me sheepishly, "I hope nothing I tell you here can be used against me, detective."

"Don't worry about it," I told him, as I looked around the room at the shelves full of books. "Why don't you tell me about these? The books. What makes them so special, so valuable?"

Spear quickly brightened, "Why, Detective Hollow, I'd be happy to. I could see you have an interest in collecting, but knew it was not books."

"No, not books, Depression Glassware," I said.

"Ah, yes, Jadite, Fenton, Carnival, and such?"

"Yes, but I'm getting interested in books. Can you teach me about them?" I prompted.

"That's a tall order. There's so much to tell," Spears began but with obvious enthusiasm. "I mean, books are wonderful, endlessly fascinating. Take a look at some of the ones I have here on the shelves. Go ahead, pull one out, take a look."

I did as he said. I looked over the bound edges of the books that were facing me on the shelves, what I had learned was called the spine of the book. These spines showed the names of titles and authors. Some of the names I recognized. I saw a copy of James M. Cain's *The Postman Always Rings Twice* and pulled it out. "I remember the movie with Lana Turner and John Garfield."

"Yeah, she was a real peach in her day. The film was from 1946. That book is the first edition, from Knopf in 1934. It's lightly cocked, but otherwise in fine condition, you picked a good book."

"Did I?" I asked, showing my surprise. I had no idea.

"Yes, the jacket is what makes it, it's in lovely condition. I value it at about $6,000. I have a buyer, or at least, someone seriously interested. Another dealer, drat! If I resell it to him, I'll have to give him the standard twenty percent discount to the trade. I'd rather sell it to a collector at the full price but maybe it is time for it to go."

"I see. I looked the book over. The jacket didn't seem to be much, just some fancy lettering of the title with smaller letters at the lower edge of the author's name. I put it back on the shelf. Then I reached over and picked up a small book that was near it, a paperback, a very old paperback."

"That's interesting, do you know what you have there?"

I shrugged, "I haven't the faintest idea. *The Good Earth* by Pearl Buck, right?"

Spears laughed, genuinely happy to talk books and I had to admit his enthusiasm was getting to me, "Yes, but it is a very special book. Actually it is an historical artifact, an icon of American publishing."

"Really?" I was interested but skeptical. I mean, it was just a paperback.

"That's because it's the very *first* mass-market paperback ever. In 1939 Simon & Schuster partnered with Robert de Graff to publish Pocket Books, which began the Paperback Revolution, which spread like wildfire across the country, and then across the world. All Pocket Books were numbered. The number run reached over a thousand, much higher even. Look at the spine. Do you see any number?"

I turned the book and looked at the bound edge, the spine. "No, there's no number."

"That's right!" Spears almost shouted in his excitement. "In 1939 Pocket Books published a tiny trial edition of that book with no number, only 2,000 copies that were given away to influential persons, and distributed only in New York City. There are less than a dozen copies known to exist today."

"What's the value of something like that?" I asked, not very impressed. I mean, it didn't look like much of a book to me. And it was just a paperback. I didn't think paperbacks were worth anything. Coupla dollars, maybe?

"Well, it is worth perhaps $5,000. It's a very nice copy," Spears said with a smile at my evident surprise.

I carefully put it back on his shelf.

"That much, for just a paperback?"

"Oh, yes, and you'd be surprised to know that many paperbacks go for big money these days. Not as much as hardcover firsts of course, but in the hundreds of dollars and sometimes in the thousands of dollars. There is a very frantic market for certain paperbacks. You know about first editions?"

"Yes, that is the first time a book has appeared in print, right?" I answered carefully. At that point I wasn't so sure of what I knew and something told me the old guy was going to throw me a curve.

"Correct, but many collectible authors, many famous books, originally appeared in paperback. These are called, appropriately enough, paperback originals. These paperbacks are the first true editions. Many famous genre writers got their start in the forties, fifties and sixties in paperback, so you'll find a lot of key mystery, crime, science fiction and horror work that originally appeared in paperback. These are avidly collected by fans. Paperbacks also have better cover art than hardcover books, much more sexy, passionate, violent, much more exciting overall—and that's exciting to collectors. There are even books published that reproduce the best paperback cover art. The artists have their own followings too."

I sighed, I had a lot to learn. I looked over at the shelves again. "You have some very expensive books here."

"Yes, but these books did not just appear one day, mysteriously. They are the result of a lifetime of collecting, a lifetime in books, my friend. I buy everywhere I can, I search constantly, it is fun, part of the joy of collecting. The hunt!"

"I know that feeling."

"I am sure you do, from your glass collecting, certainly. Well, I hunt and buy from other dealer lists, book shows, yard sales, flea markets, thrift stores, and the best when I can get them, estate sales. It is great fun and gives me much joy, and it has given me a decent living doing something I love. What can be better?"

I noticed another book and pulled it down to look at it more closely.

"Ah, yes, the Steinbeck, that's a very nice copy. It took me a lot of work to get that one. I got it from an old collector who bought it new when it first came out in 1939. It was a real job to get him to part with it and I think I overpaid, but I'm not bothered by that now. It's in lovely condition, a hint of foxing, but the jacket is glorious, so I am well pleased with it."

"*The Grapes of Wrath*," I said, looking over the jacket art showing Oakie farmers during the Depression. What's something like this worth?"

"I conservatively estimate it at $20,000."

I grimaced and put the book back on the shelf. "This is a bit overwhelming."

Spears laughed, "It can be, there is a lot to learn, a lot to know. I've been in the business for over thirty years and every day I learn something new. The important thing as a dealer is that selling books is my bread and butter, so I don't want to get caught with my pants down."

I smiled, "What do you mean?"

"No one can know everything. Smarties abound, but

always get outsmarted. Every dealer has their interests and specialty, but when they come across something outside that realm they can become nervous, they have to be careful."

"I know what you mean: you can sell too cheap if you don't know what you have. It's the same with glassware," I said, remembering the competitiveness there for prime pieces among dealers.

"Correct. It can be a bit of a crap shoot, but a pleasant one. I could think of no other way to spend my time on this old world of ours," Spears said softly, thoughtful now. "But what do you like to read? Do you have a favorite book, a favorite author?"

I sighed, "Police work doesn't give me much time for reading. I like private eye stories, Dashiell Hammett, Raymond Chandler, crime fiction generally, and some science fiction and horror."

"Hammett, Chandler, probably Stephen King, perhaps in science fiction, Isaac Asimov?"

"Yeah, he wrote *The Foundation Trilogy*, didn't he? I read them in school."

Al Spears got up and walked over to the shelf behind him, pulling down three hardcover books wrapped in clear shiny plastic. "Here they are, Asimov's Foundation Trilogy: *Foundation, Foundation and Empire* and *Second Foundation*."

He handed me the books and I looked at the jacket art. They showed spaceships and alien faces. They were lovely and the condition was really nice, almost like new. "These must be old. I remember these covers from when I was a kid, from the high school library."

"Not these books, Detective Hollow, but ones just like them, reprints certainly, or book club editions, which abound. These are the first editions from Gnome Press, a small science fiction specialty publisher. They were published one each year, from 1951 to 1953 and these copies have the added bonus of being signed by the author."

"Do signed books bring a higher price?" I asked.

"Good question. That depends on the author. Asimov did sign quite a bit. Other authors don't sign much, some won't. Others, sadly, die young. Unfortunately, the signature on most books contributes little if nothing to its overall value."

"So Asimov signed these? Are they worth more signed."

"For Asimov, absolutely. You see, while Asimov signed a lot of books, he's a revered science fiction writer, a real icon, and these three books are his magnum opus. You know, he also wrote sequels back in the '80s and the '90s before he died; later, other writers continued the series, but these three were the originals. There is significant demand. They are science fiction cornerstones as well. I'd place them easily at $5,000 a piece, perhaps as much as $20,000 for the set of three."

"Wow!" I blurted, in spite of myself. It was amazing, the world of rare books was like an entire new world that had suddenly opened up before me. I was just glad that Charlie Grant wasn't here. My moron partner would just be annoyed by all this book talk, and I didn't want anything to interfere with my newly acquired fascination for books. I carefully handed Spears back his Asimovs.

"Nice, eh?" he asked me with a glint to his eyes as he took the books and placed them back on his shelf.

"Yeah, but nothing I can afford."

Spears nodded sagely, "Yes, that is true for now, but not always, and there are great finds still out there. All you have to do is look. You'd be surprised. You just have to know what to look for."

"That's just it, I don't know what to look for."

Spears smiled, "Yes you do, you have an advisor."

"I do?"

"Of course, you have me. I'll teach you what you need to know. That is, if you really want to learn."

I thought about that carefully. It was very generous of him, but I was still on a case. I was a busy cop with a messy career, a runaway wife. I really didn't need another job on top of all that, especially one that seemed so complicated. I had no idea how to be a bookman, what to look for, even with the help of Al Spears.

"I don't know," I said almost sadly.

"Well, maybe some day, Detective Hollow. I can see you have the collecting bug in you, and you seem to have a real interest in books. I think that some day, we will meet again…in books."

"I hope so, Mr. Spears. Thanks for all your time, I enjoyed it and I think I learned a few things."

"Well, then our time hasn't been wasted. Good luck, detective.

We shook hands and I got ready to leave. I took one last look at the books filling the shelves all around me. They were magical. It was really quite nice to look at them all, and I didn't even notice the cat smell any longer.

On the way out Spears walked me to the door. That's when the attack came. It was fast and furious. I was ambushed by that damn Hemingway. The cat clawed my hand as I fought him off and sent him scampering away. I think he had been going for my gun.

* * * * * * *

The doorbell rang and it was answered right away.

"You? What do you want?"

"Good morning. I have something for you. Something I know you are looking for very much. I have it here in this box."

"What is it?"

"You'll see. Will you let me in?"

"You're the last person I expected to see."

"I'm sure, but do you want what I have here, or not?"

"What is it?"

"Are you going to let me in?"

"Very well."

"Let's go upstairs, into Brian's old office, where we can be alone. Is anyone else in the house.

"No."

"The maid, or your pool boy, perhaps?"

"They're all gone, off for the day, and my sister

and mother have gone back home. They were getting annoying. We're quite alone."

"That's good, then lead the way upstairs."

"All right, follow me. You know, I am surprised to see you. It has been a long time."

"Yes, it has."

"Here we are, Brian's old office. Come in."

"This is the room where Brian was murdered?"

"Yes. He was killed there, right at that very desk."

"How awful."

"Yes, it was a surprise, let me tell you."

"I read it in all the papers. It must have been very difficult for you."

"Well, we were going to divorce, so…."

"Of course."

"So what do you have for me?"

"It's here in this box. Take it and open it. See for yourself."

"All right. Let me see. Well…it's a book of some kind. Some kind of binder."

"Not just any old binder."

"My God! It's Brian's missing Value Book…."

"Yes, it is."

"I've been looking everywhere for this!"

"Well now you have it back."

"But…but that means…doesn't that mean you took it? Then that means…you're Brian's murderer!"

"Yes. It does."

Then two shots were fired, a body fell to the floor, and the visitor quickly left the empty house. It was not yet noon.

* * * * * * *

It was noon and I called Charlie Grant to compare notes.

"I spoke to Spears," I told my partner over my cell phone. "He's a good guy. He's pretty upset about McDonald using his name, he was highly insulted and worried about how it will all play out."

"Huh! Too bad. I still think he's in deeper than he lets on. What about all those names he gave us?"

"Spears told me he knew some of the people, used some of the libraries for research on occasion, like all book people do. I don't think there's much to it though."

"That's it, Hollow, you don't think," Grant jibbed.

I let it go, counted to ten, then said, "So what did you come up with?"

"I visited the two Black women. The ex-maid, Sledge, is a nasty piece of work, she told me McDonald owed her big time for getting her fired. She had a sweet gig, from what she told me. She did nothing at all, just serviced the bookman for pay and perks. Live-in hooker. Nice set-up! Then the wife caught her and McDonald doing the dirty deed in the upstairs bedroom—the same bedroom where hubby and wife slept, not a good idea. Sledge was fired. McDonald ended up dumping her soon after. Our boy had no scruples, no loyalty at all."

"Yeah, he was one of a kind."

Grant continued, "Then I ran by to see the mistress,

Alice Sparks. She seems to have moved on from McDonald, wanted nothing to do with him after a brief affair. Seems she dumped him a month or two ago. She wasn't all that interested in him anyway, just his money, and when the money got sparse, so did she. She's an interesting woman."

"How so?"

"Well, she came on to me," he said simply.

I was surprised and could imagine the leering smile on Grant's face. I resisted the urge to comment or ask for explicit details.

"Don't you want to hear about it?" he prompted.

"Not really."

Grant was quiet for a moment, obviously disappointed I had not jumped to the bait to hear about his most recent sexual adventure.

"So what now, Hollow?"

"I guess we finish it up. You revisit the wife, see what she has to say, I'll drop in on the ex-wife again, see what I can come up with there."

"Zilch, is all," he said, then hung up.

CHAPTER NINE

Brian McDonald's ex-wife was Sandy Goddard and I remembered her all right from our first visit with her days before. Amazon-big, a figure that didn't quit, very nice looking all ways around. She was still hanging on as a real peach at her age, looking very good, even into her forties. Not bad at all. I didn't mind this part of the job.

Since Beth had left me I'd been lonely and horny and that's no way for any man to go through life. I figured for once I'd got the better assignment here, at least it was the most pleasant, even though Goddard had admitted to us she was a lesbian. She had no interest in men but at least she seemed to be a pleasant person. Certainly an interesting woman to be around. Not that I was like Grant. I didn't expect anything, other than a decent conversation with her. Which was okay by me. Goddard seemed to be a far better person than her replacement in McDonald's sordid life—that cold and nasty bitch, Milly. I figured, let Grant talk to Milly all he liked. He was welcomed to her and her cold attitude. I got a chill just thinking about that one.

I had called ahead and Goddard buzzed me up to her

apartment. The building and her rooms weren't much to look at, but she sure was. Charlie Grant and I had been here a few days before. Her place was the same sparse environment, not much furniture, just a couch and one recliner surrounding a glass-topped coffee table. No entertainment center, no TV, but there was a small wet bar against the far wall. I guess she couldn't afford much, just the essentials. Then again, maybe she didn't need or want anything else.

"Detective Hollow," Goddard said, and a brief smile came to her face as she let me into her apartment. She was dressed in a tight pair of slacks with a halter top that didn't hide her female assets at all. I gulped nervously, this was going to be a lot more difficult than I had first thought. I realized I'd have to keep my libido in check, focus on the job at hand, and remember there was no possibility of anything coming of this whatso-ever. She was a lesbian after all, so the only thing sexu-ally that could come of this was frustration. Well, I'd been married to Beth for years, so I was used to sexual frustration.

"Hello, Ms. Goddard," I said returning her smile. "Thanks for seeing me on such short notice."

"You can call me Sandy," she said, and there was that mild smile again, as she lead me into the living room and over to the couch. "Drink?"

"No, I'd better not. Not while on duty."

She laughed rather gaily, and I though, well now, how apropos is that?

"So where's your partner?"

"He's working another part of the case."

"So he won't be coming here?" she asked. Did I see a glint in her eye?

"No."

"That's good, because I don't like him. If you don't mind me saying it, he's a real asshole."

I laughed out loud, rather surprised by my spontaneity but enjoying this bit of mirth at Grant's expense. She joined in with me, with a deep throaty laugh that told me she'd had a lot of practice and enjoyed being joyful. It was nice. It was also the first good laugh I'd had in days, weeks, maybe months.

"You have a nice laugh, detective, do you know that?" she offered, there was that wan smile again. "You like to laugh, don't you?"

"Yeah, when I can find something to laugh about."

"But you don't laugh nearly enough, not like you should. Why is that, Detective Hollow?" she asked me, and I felt something tighten deep within me, tugging at my heart. Was it sadness? Loneliness? Life's realization of all that had been lost?

I looked at her carefully, she looked so nice as she stood there over me with that wan smile, but I began to wonder. What game was she playing? Was she coming on to me? Was she even playing any game at all? I shrugged, probably not. My thoughts went back to what she had said about Grant; that he was an asshole. I smiled, "You know, you're right about Grant."

"How could you work with such a moron?"

"Let me tell you, it hasn't been easy, but the brass

partnered us together so he and I have no choice. If it's any consolation, Grant dislikes me as much as I dislike him."

"Oh, I can't believe that, detective," then she finished mixing herself a drink and plopped herself down next to me on the couch. She was close, not touching me, but close. I could feel the heat off her body; I could smell the light scent of her perfume. She looked at me and smiled.

"You can call me Sandy," she said, adding, "and Detective Hollow sounds so formal. What is your first name?"

"Bentley."

She laughed, "Well, that's certainly...."

"My friends call me Ben," I offered quickly.

"Ben, yes, I like that. That's a lot better. Okay, Ben, it's good to see you again. What can I do for you?"

I switched into full cop mode, all serious, "Just a few questions."

"About Brian?" she asked, which seemed odd to me because whatever else would I be there to ask her about?

"Yes, Brian," I said softly. Was it getting hot in her apartment, or was it just her? Was the air conditioning working right? I looked over at the vent. Yes, it was still blowing cold air into the room. It was late afternoon and a fairly warm day, but it seemed to be getting warmer by the minute.

"Maybe I'll take that drink now," I said with a smile.

"...Sandy?" she prompted.

"Ah, maybe I'll take that drink now, Sandy."

She smiled back at me rather delightfully, I thought, which seemed odd. She said, "Well, that's better."

Then she stood up and walked over to the bar. When she got up I watched her move, the sway and shape of her body. Man, she was all woman, female poetry in motion, and she knew it and flaunted it. What a shame she was not only out of my league but not even interested in my gender. Oh well, my bad luck. I watched her joyfully anyway, enjoying the view. I think she knew I was looking at her. It probably got her ego going. I didn't mind, it got me going too.

"What will you have, Ben?"

"Oh, gin and tonic, light on the gin, with ice if you have it, please."

She fixed the drink and brought it over to me with a sly wink. I sighed, what did that wink mean? Probably nothing. Then she handed me the glass and sat down next to me. Did I miss something or was she sitting closer to me now than she had before?

"I hope you like the drink."

"I'm sure I will." I took a sip. "Yes, that hits the spot."

"Good. So what do you want to talk to me about, Ben?"

Every time she spoke now she said my name, she smiled at me, then moved closer to me. Nothing overly blatant, you understand, just mild teasing, but she came a little bit closer each time.

We were touching now. I could feel the heat off her body, drink in the scent of her perfume and I could feel myself becoming aroused. That was not good. I mean, it was good, but it shouldn't be happening. Stuff like that never happens to me. I mean, I was on police business—a damn murder case no less, of which I reminded myself her ex-husband had been the victim. Here I was falling for one of the witnesses—and one I could never have. Oh, she was a fine tease, I'll give her that, but it was all just so damn frustrating. She was a lesbian, so she was off limits to me, a waste of my time. Grant had been right after all.

She moved closer, somehow, and said, "I like you, Ben, you know that?"

I looked into her eyes and she was smiling at me softly. Her hand suddenly rested on my knee. It did not move. Neither did I.

I looked back at her, a bit surprised. "Ah, Sandy... Ms. Goddard...are you...are you coming on to me?" Even as I uttered the words I felt like a fool, allowing my fantasies to get the better of me with her teasing. I was immediately sorry that I had let the cat out of the bag about my own feelings towards her. I was acting like a real moron. Like Grant, or worse! I awaited the inevitable reply, some suitably sarcastic and biting retort, probably with the word 'pathetic' in it. I felt suddenly sad, and very lonely. Well, I deserved it. What she said next really did shock me and it had me fumbling for a reply.

"And what if I am, Ben?" she said plainly, her hand still upon my knee, her eyes looking into my own, her mouth slightly open and the red moist lips barely inches from my own.

"But you're…a lesbian!" I blurted, like some damn schoolboy.

She just laughed, "If you must know the truth, I'm not a very good lesbian, Ben. Maybe I'm just a part-timer."

"Part-timer? What does that mean? Is there such a thing?"

"I sour on men like Brian and move onto women, but then I sour on women and always come back to men when I find one that interests me," she said, her hand moving up my leg as my lips moved onto hers. "It gets so boring. I'd like to find a man I can have something meaningful with. Can you be that man, Ben?"

I was in a trance, confused but delighted. Stuff just happens like that sometimes—but never to me. Whoever would have thought it, certainly not I. Not Bentley Hollow. I bent down to kiss her and her lips met mine. We tussled on the couch for a while, undressing each other and then we made our way into her bedroom down the hall.

It was a busy afternoon let me tell you. It had been months since Beth had left me, with no one in between, so it had been a long stretch for me to go without. I had a lot of pent-up feelings to release and it appeared Sandy felt the same way. We released each other wonderfully.

"You know, I haven't been with a man since Brian," she told me before we really got down to serious love-making. "Please be gentle with me."

I laughed and she gave me a pouting look back. It

was lovely.

"You be gentle with me, I haven't been with a woman since my wife left me months ago—and even then we didn't—you know—for a long time."

"We've both been ill-treated in love, Ben," she stated. "Now is our turn to make up for it."

I kissed her hard, I guess she was right.

* * * * * * *

An hour or so later we were both pretty well spent. She was lying naked upon the sheets, dead to the world, but looking very satisfied. I had to smile, I felt pretty good myself. *Hollow, you old dog, you still got it.*

I was up now, butt naked, getting out of the bed because of a call coming in on my cell. I'd set the phone to vibrate and thrown it to the floor and forgot all about it while Sandy and I had got down to the business of lovemaking. Now I noticed it was humming at me wildly demanding a response. I shook my head annoyed at the interruption, then quickly picked up my cell phone from the pile of my clothes—I was, after all, still on a case.

I quickly went into the living room so as not to disturb Sandy. She was sleeping dreamily like she didn't have a care in the world. She looked so damn pretty.

"Hollow? Hollow, you there?" The voice at the other end of the phone barked rapidly, impatient.

I sighed, "Yeah, Grant, what do you want?"

"Been trying to call you for the last hour. You had your phone off?"

"No," I lied. "I must be in a dead zone."

"Yeah, dead zone, my ass. Where the hell are you?"

"The ex-wife's place. So what do you want?" I said trying to hold my patience. I was standing in Sandy's living room stark naked, talking low so as not to wake her as I talked to my moron partner. I wondered what Grant wanted now.

"Listen, Hollow, I went to see the wife like we planned. She's dead. I found her shot twice. Looks like it was done early this morning. The crime scene guys and the Captain are on their way over. You'd better make a beeline here, pronto!" Grant ordered.

Milly McDonald dead? Murdered? I shook my head to clear it, trying to think this through.

"Okay, Grant, thanks for the heads-up," I said grateful to my idiot partner as I tried to absorb the shock of this new development in the case and what it might mean.

I shook my head and shut the phone. I had to get dressed and out of there fast, but I didn't want to wake Sandy. Not just yet. I remember how she looked in bed, so peaceful in her lust-induced slumber, so lovely in her lush nakedness.

I walked out of the living room and down the hall to go back into her bedroom to get my clothes and get dressed. On the way I had to take a leak so I looked for the bathroom. I opened the first closed door off that hallway, but it wasn't the bathroom just another bedroom—a room I'd never been in before. Then I froze. The room was surrounded by wooden shelves on all four walls and upon those shelves were books. A lot of books. Books everywhere!

I was stunned. I looked inside amazed and then walked around the room looking at all the volumes of what looked like expensive first editions. It was a relatively small grouping of books, but it looked like primo stuff. Some pretty old and nice condition editions, I assumed all were first editions.

I was intrigued, but initially, that was all I felt. After all, Sandy had been married to a major book dealer for years, she was also an intelligent, educated woman, so it was quite natural, maybe even essential, that she would have books in her place. Maybe even a lot of books.

Then I saw it!

The thick binder laying on the middle of the desktop all by itself. I could hardly have missed it. It was the same description as Brian McDonald's missing Value Book. I walked over slowly, nervously, well aware of just what it might mean if this was in fact McDonald's missing book. Could it be?

Nah, I told myself. No, it had to be a coincidence. Maybe Sandy had her own record book, maybe she'd even taken the idea from her former husband? Hadn't Spears told me all serious dealers and collectors had such a book or kept such records? That made sense. That had to be it, I thought. That would be normal, not a coincidence—but a little voice inside me told me it was otherwise. What it told me I just didn't want to believe.

Even as I opened the binder and read what was written there I knew the truth of it all now.

I was startled by the voice that came from behind me.

"So you found it, Ben," Sandy said bluntly, and I turned to see her standing there totally nude, her lovely ripe body framed in the doorway, a gun in her hand leveled right at me.

I signed, deflated with disappointment more than fear, not knowing how to react, so I asked the obvious question, "You killed Brian?"

"Yes, I did, Ben, and I also shot that bitch Milly. The world's a better place without her. I should get a medal for that one, let me tell you. You'll hear about Milly soon. I'm sure it will make the news."

"Grant just called me about it, he found her body an hour ago," I told her, hardly noticing her nudity now, or my own. It was almost ludicrous, me standing there totally buck naked in a room full of rare books while a lovely "part-time" lesbian I'd just made love to stood totally naked before me—the gun in her hand leveled at me was the only sobering equation in that crazy scene.

"So what now?" I asked, my eyes drifting from the lovely nakedness of her firm bounteous breasts, over to the moistness of her womanhood, and then locking on that damn gun she had pointed at me.

"I don't know, Ben," she said plainly. I could see genuine sadness in her features, maybe even a tear of regret streaming down her cheek. "Why the hell did you have to snoop around? Why the hell did you come in here? I had the door closed, you shouldn't have opened it."

"I was looking for the bathroom," I said lamely.

She laughed lightly, smiled delightfully at that. "Men!"

I said, "Sandy, are you going to kill me too? You know you won't get away with this now."

"I know that, Ben."

"Why don't you give me the gun?"

She pointed it at me hard then, fire came into her eyes, "No. I have to think about this. I have to think…."

I tried another tack. "Why did you do it? Why did you kill Brian, and why did you write that message on his desk, 'Book Collector's, Go to Hell!'?"

She moved the gun so it centered on my heart, not a good sign.

"He not only cheated on me with other women, which was bad enough, I could handle that. What I couldn't handle was that he cheated me out of my father's books in the divorce settlement."

"You father's books?" I blurted not understanding what she was telling me and showing it in my face.

She smiled indulgently, explained, "When we were married I brought my father's books to the marriage which were combined with Brian's. My father had a very valuable collection and I inherited them upon his death."

"But you told Grant and me you didn't collect anything, especially books!"

She smiled sweetly, "I lied, Ben. A woman's provocative. I didn't have to tell you and that other detective my personal business."

"So Brian screwed you in the divorce settlement?"

"Yes and no. He wanted all the books so he gave me the house and some cash. At the time it seemed like a good deal—all I was giving up was my father's musty old books. Who cared about them? Certainly not I, at the time," she admitted sadly. "Then I found out just how much they were worth. Brian built his business on the books he stole from me. My father's books. I know I gave them up, I know I should have been more knowledgeable about their value—but he was my husband, Ben. I trusted him. When he told me they were not worth all that much I believed him. They were just dad's old books, to me. At that time I never took an interest in books or the book business."

"I see."

"I trusted Brian. He should have let me know their true value and given me a fair price for them, instead he had all that information locked away in his damn secret Value Book. Then during the divorce he gave me a settlement that looked generous, as long as he kept all the books. The books were all that he ever really wanted. It wasn't fair. I wanted them back."

"So he not only stole from you. I heard he stole from everyone. You know that he stole from some university libraries and their special collections also?"

"The bastard!"

"Then why do Milly McDonald?" I asked carefully.

We were standing there stark naked, but any sexual interest had long since diminished and been lost. The gun she held pointed at me I now realized was probably the very weapon she had used to murder McDonald's wife bare hours earlier that morning.

"That greedy bitch! If I wasn't going to allow Brian to get away with keeping all my father's—now my—rare and valuable books, there was no way in hell I was going to let Milly get them all. I knew about the divorce, so I knew I had to act fast before the books were split up. That would make things too difficult. I had to act while they were all in one place. Milly was not a good and trusting soul like me, Ben. She would have made sure she got half the books, probably the better half, if I knew her like I thought I did. I had no choice but to act before that happened."

"Give me the gun, Sandy," I said firmly.

She just laughed, "You look so funny there, Ben, totally naked, with your shriveled little pishee and all."

I allowed a wan grin, what could I say about that?

"Ben. I'm so sorry." Then she added softly, "I guess I made a mess out of everything."

All I saw now were her hard eyes looking at me and the barrel of that gun pointed straight at my heart.

"You don't want to do this, Sandy," I pleaded, trying to hide the fear I felt and the desperation in my voice. "You don't want to kill me. You'll never get away with it."

"I know that," she replied softly, like she was already in a far away place and it was our last goodbye. She gave me a sad little smile, "I'll miss you, Ben, I really will. I just want you to know that. But what I wrote is true, book collectors do go to hell, sometimes."

She looked at me firmly, eye to eye. I could see the determination in her now. It was scary. I knew she had made a hard decision to cut her loses and that it was coming to fruition very soon.

I shuddered, tightly closed my eyes and waited. Then I heard the shot. The single report seemed to last a lifetime and it reverberated throughout the small room, echoing off all the shelves filled so tightly with so many books.

I stood there frozen, in panic and astonishment. Then I opened my eyes and saw Sandy's lush body fall to the floor with a hard thump, the pistol dropping from her limp fingers. Blood spurted from a wound in her temple.

"Sandy!" I shouted. "Sandy! No!"

She looked at me strangely as I ran over to her and cradled her head in my arms, the blood madly gushing like a stream over our bodies. Her eyes looked blank, dull, I knew she was slipping away. Then she suddenly focused on me for an instant and a brief smile came to her lips, "Ben...I do like you...," she whispered, "and I guess you do care."

"Yes, I do," I spoke softly, between my tears. "Sandy? Sandy!"

I cried as she died there in my arms. I lay there with her for hours, the two of us naked, wrapped together with her blood all over our bodies. I hardly noticed it.

I couldn't move, I didn't know what to do. My police training wanted to kick in—I know what I should have done—but I just couldn't do it.

I cried a lot that night and I let myself sleep in her dead arms.

* * * * * * *

They found us early the next morning. They came for me when I never showed at the McDonald house. Charlie Grant was the first one to come into the room and see us, then Captain Wallace and the crime scene team.

I vaguely remember seeing Grant looking down at us with shock, then an evil twisted leer came to his face when he saw our nakedness.

"My God, Hollow, where the hell are your clothes?" Grant said looking at my nakedness and then grinning. "What the hell you do, man, fuck her to death!"

The crime scene team took their photos, then one of them helped me up from Sandy's body. Then they took more photos of her alone. One of the guys dropped a towel over me and then sat me in a chair.

I looked at Charlie Grant with rage and unabashed hatred. This partnership was about to end—right now—the hard way.

Charlie Grant came over to me, a sly, wicked grin on his face.

"So tell me, what was she like?"

I stood up from my chair and suddenly hit Grant with a brick-hard fist straight into his face. It was a pile-driver blow that must have broken his nose—blood was spurting everywhere from his face—he rolled over and cried like a baby.

"This partnership is over!" I shouted, closing the subject forever.

I looked at Captain Wallace, he'd witnessed the entire scene, as well as all the crime scene techs. I was in the shit now. I realized this had not been such a good career move but it felt so damn good I didn't care just then.

"You'll find Brian McDonald's missing Value Book on her desk there. It proves Sandy Goddard was the killer of Brian McDonald, her gun will match the bullets that killed Milly McDonald also."

Then, still stark naked, I calmly walked out of the room and down the hall into Sandy's bedroom. I gathered my clothes. I ignored the blood on me. It was Sandy's blood. It was the only thing I had left from her now. As I got dressed Captain Wallace came into the bedroom.

He looked at me for a long moment in utter shock. I looked back hard, daring him to speak. Finally he did.

"This is a real mess, Hollow," he told me, not without some sympathy, but I could see he had a job to do and no nonsense could be allowed now. "You found the killer and closed the case, which is good. You did a good job, but your methods are damn irregular...."

"You mean sleeping with a witness?"

"Sleeping with the murderer, Hollow," he corrected me with a sharp stare.

I thought it was a minor point to remind Wallace that at the time we had begun to make love Sandy had only been a witness, so I said nothing. I'd never thought of her as a suspect and certainly not a murderer.

Wallace looked at me grimly, shook his head sadly and continued, "When this gets out, and it will, Hollow, it will cause all kinds of unpleasantness in the media for me, and for the department. I think it might be best…."

"Don't worry yourself about it, Captain," I said as I put on my pants and tucked in my shirt. "I've got the time, I'm putting in my papers. I'll be gone by the end of the week."

"That might be best, Hollow," he said with a deep sigh of relief, and just a hint of regret.

"I know it will be," I replied and walked out of the bedroom, leaving him standing there alone. On the way out I shouted back to him, "You need me for anything, you know how to reach me. You'll have a written statement from me in a couple of days. Now, I'm going home. I've had enough. Enough of Charlie Grant, enough of you, enough of this damn department, and enough of being a cop."

ABOUT THE AUTHOR

GARY LOVISI is a Mystery Writers of America Edgar Award nominee. His latest books are *Dames, Dolls & Delinquents*, a collector's guide to sexy pulp fiction paperbacks (Krause, 2009) and *Bad Girls Need Love Too* (Krause, 2010), which will appear as an off-Broadway stage play in New York City in 2011. His hard crime novels include *Hellbent on Homicide* and *Blood in Brooklyn* (Do Not Press, UK), and the hard crime and noir collection, *Ultra-Boiled* (Ramble House Books, 2010). Lovisi is the founder of Gryphon Books, editor of *Paperback Parade* and *Hardboiled* magazines, and the sponsor of an annual book collector show in New York City. To find out more about him, his work, or Gryphon Books, visit his web site at:

www.gryphonbooks.com

THE PAPERBACK
SHOW MURDERS

When Courtlandt Frederick van Noland ("Freddie the Cur" to his enemies—he has no friends) is found stabbed through the heart with a pen at his dealer's table at the 50th Paperback Exposition and Show in Santo Verdugo, Calif., Police Lieutenant Pfisch is forced to close the con. After all, this is the third untimely death of the show's attendees in as many days.

First there was feminist bookseller Lissa Boaz, called "The Boa Constrictor" for her questionable business practices. Then came Brody Richard "The O-Man" Dameen, the drunken horror writer, now reduced to peddling his memoirs and begging for money.

What links the victims, other than rare and collectible paperbacks? And why does the identification of the *real* author of an early Ace gothic novel even matter? A comic mystery novel of the modern con scene.

Selected Borgo Press Books by ROBERT REGINALD

Academentia: A Future Dystopia
Ancestral Voices: An Anthology of Early Science Fiction
Ancient Hauntings (ed. with Douglas Menville)
The Attempted Assassination of John F. Kennedy
BP 300: A Bibliography of the Borgo Press, 1976-1998
Choice Words: Writers Writing About Writing (editor)
Classics of Fantastic Literature (with Douglas Menville)
Codex Derynianus III (with Katherine Kurtz)
The Dark-Haired Man; or, The Hieromonk's Tale (NE #1)
Dreamers of Dreams (ed. with Douglas Menville)
The Exiled Prince; or, The Archquisitor's Tale (NE #2)
Forgotten Fantasy: Issues #1-5 (ed. with Douglas Menville)
The Fourth Elephant's Egg; or, The Hypatomancer's Tale (#4)
"A Glorious Death": The Human-Knacker War, Book Three
The House of the Burgesses (with Mary A. Burgess)
If J.F.K. Had Lived (with Jeffrey M. Elliot)
Invasion! Earth vs. the Aliens (War of Two Worlds #1)
The Judgment of the Gods and Other Verdicts of History
King Solomon's Children (ed. with Douglas Menville)
Knack' Attack: A Tale of the Human-Knacker War (Book Two)
The Martians Strike Back! (War of Two Worlds #3)
The Nasty Gnomes: A Novel of the Phantom Detective (#2)
Operation Crimson Storm (War of Two Worlds #2)
The Paperback Show Murders
Phantasmagoria (ed. with Douglas Menville)
The Phantom's Phantom: A Novel of the Phantom Detective—#1
Quæstiones; or, The Protopresbyter's Tale (Nova Europa #3)
R.I.P. (ed. with Douglas Menville)
The Spectre Bridegroom and Other Horrors (ed. with Menville)
They (ed. with Douglas Menville)
Trilobite Dreams; or, The Autodidact's Tale: An Autobiography
Worlds of Never (ed. with Douglas Menville)
Xenograffiti: Essays on Fantastic Literature

THE PAPERBACK
SHOW MURDERS

ROBERT REGINALD

THE BORGO PRESS
MMXI

THE PAPERBACK SHOW MURDERS

FIRST EDITION

Published by Wildside Press LLC

www.wildsidebooks.com

DEDICATION

To the memory of my dear friend,

Allan Aaron Adrian
(23 January 1931 - 4 October 2009)

Bookhound extraordinaire;

Also for **Doug Menville** *and* **Barry Levin**,

And our now ancient adventures
Trolling Booksellers' Row in Hollywood;

And to all the eccentric proprietors of all the
Odd little bookshops that I've encountered
Over the years—most of them, lamentably,
Now permanently out-of-print.

AUTHOR'S NOTE

There's no resemblance intended, of course, between the Fiftieth Paperback Exposition and Show at Santo Verdugo, California, and the Annual Paperback Collectors Show & Sale at Mission Hills, California, although Mary and I have enjoyed our occasional presence at the latter. None of the invented authors or bookmongers or attendees featured herein are intended to mimic, mock, or resemble any real authors or bookmongers, save for the late Donald A. Wollheim and Evelyn Grippo, both of whom I knew and respected a great deal. Indeed, I regard Don as my paradigm as an editor. Finally, Santo Verdugo is *not* San Bernardino, California, and West Highlands is *not* Highland, California, despite certain geographical similarities. All of the invented excerpts from supposed vintage paperbacks are solely my creation, and you may cringe and/or laugh (or not), as you please.

—Robert Reginald

CONTENTS

PROLOGUE
"JUST ANOTHER DEAD BODY"

Sunday, March 27

"The corpus was sprawled like a limp sack of spuds across the plastic counter, drizzled with mounds of condiments in a vain attempt to spruce up the offering. But I knew better: this was just another course in an endless meal sweetened with fatty promises, sugar, too much salt, and a plethora of empty calories.

"I stifled a belch of indifference, and farted. To me it was just another dead body!"

—*Just Another Dead Body,*
by Robert Z. Blayd (1955)

I'd just returned from my noon-time luncheon expedition when I heard the ruckus in the other room.

"Cripes, what is it this time?" I asked Margie, who was already charging through the Johnny-burger and fried onion rings I'd brought her.

"Just another dead body, I suspect," she said, shaking her head. A piece of onion went swishing off into eter-

nity.

I left my roast beef melt and iced tea where they wouldn't damage any of our stock, and snuck into the adjoining suite, the primo dealers' display area. The crowd was thickest at the back, where "The Last Word" was located, but I couldn't tell what was happening there.

So I pushed my way through the throng, shoving aside fans and authors alike, until I could see the focus of their attention.

Finally, I spotted Courtlandt Frederick van Noland, affectionately known to his enemies as "Freddie the Cur" (he had no friends), leaning precariously back against both chair and wall, his rotund belly resting on the edge of the table that featured his display of vintage paperbacks. It looked for a moment that he was sporting a particularly long pen in his left pocket, but it was actually stuck *through* his pocket. A crimson flower was already staining the garish Hawaiian motif of his shirt.

He was quite undeniably dead, poor old Fred, and no one seemed to care very much, either.

"Well, I guess someone finally wrote him out," the well-known writer Noel G. Person said, chuckling at his semi-witticism. Person "wrote," if one can actually apply the word to such an irrepressible hack, bodice-rippers as "Makayla Sturges," SF space operas as "Cosmo Lund," and serial killer thriller-chillers as "Patterson Bates."

"Yes, they certainly canceled his subscription," the

horror writer Brand Garner said.

"He had it coming!" Levi Barton said. His dealer's table was located in the second room, the same one where I'd planted my flag.

"What's that in his left hand?" someone else asked.

Then I noticed a slim piece of paper protruding from between the dead man's clasped fingers. I looked at it more closely, but although I could tell it was a book of some sort, I couldn't make out the details.

"Why, it's the Bantam L.A. Burroughs!" Barton said, awe permeating his voice.

And no wonder! He was speaking of a bibliographic rarity issued by the short-lived company, Bantam Books of Los Angeles (not to be confused with the present publisher of that name). The West Coast Bantam was founded in 1939, and produced a short series of slim, 100-page paperbacks that sold for a dime through vending machines. It'd fallen victim in 1943 to the World War II paper shortages, and a decided lack of imagination in its cover designs.

All of the Bantam L.A. editions were rare, but the Edgar Rice Burroughs short with an illustrated cover, an abridged novel called *Tarzan in the Forbidden City*, was particularly collectible. I'd seen pictures of the book, and had sold one or two of the more common edition with the plain text covers; but had never actually encountered the pictorial version in the flesh, so to speak.

"I heard that a copy had surfaced recently," Tomás Law, one of the organizers of the con, said, "but how

did Freddie wind up with it?"

I looked at the book more closely. One of the near corners of the cover was creased. There was something peeking out from inside the pages. I dropped my head a little closer to his hand. What could it be?

And then I saw the blue words inked there. I reached out, pulled the tab away from the embracing text around it, and pocketed it.

I finally knew! I knew without a doubt who'd killed "Freddie the Cur," Lissa "The Boa Constrictor" Boaz, and Brody Richard "The O-Man" Dameen.

But…who could ever prove it?

CHAPTER ONE
"IT'S A WOMAN!"

FRIDAY, MARCH 25

"There was a monster lurking in the shadows of the carousel, a creature of crinoline and calomel, a crux ansata of all that was cruel and capricious in the world. It was ready, willing, and able to grab and gobble the first human that came near enough to its tentacles to tickle its terrible toenails.

"Suddenly it lurched towards me, its twin peaks jutting out into the stark, raving light.

"'It's a woman!' someone screamed—and I knew right then that this particular poltergeist wasn't going to be any pushover!"

—*The Devil's in the Details,*
by Bosco Wolfstein (1958)

The fiftieth Paperback Exposition and Show was touted as a grander version of the one-day event that sprang forth in Southern California with the advent of spring each year. The venue was completely new: a

well-worn motel called The Royal Crest in south San-to Verdugo, California, a bad-boy town celebrating its bicentennial that year.

For the con's golden anniversary, the event would be spread over a three-day period, with many more signing sessions by many more writers. The brochure promised to resurrect some vintage authors who hadn't been seen in years (or decades, in a few cases).

The book dealers, of course, knew that the larger audience generated by these extra appearances would mean increased sales of their crumbling wares, the luridly dressed mass market paperbacks of the 1940s, '50s, and '60s. So, in spite of the recession, the three large display rooms quickly sold out. Margie and I were very lucky indeed to secure a back wall in Dealer Room B.

We'd put together some of our best offerings in years. I'd managed to assemble a complete run of the mid-1960s reprints of the forty-eight pulp magazine classics issued by Corinth Books, an imprint of the notorious (by the standards of the day) porn publisher, Greenleaf Books of San Diego. In "Near Mint" condition, these were well worth the $1,000 price I'd posted, and I had no doubt they'd sell very close to that level as a set.

Individual gems included Lambert Wilhelm's porn SF spoof, *Starship Intercourse* (priced at a cool grand all by its lonesome—and signed by the author!); Bob Silverstein's werewolf porn (I'd bumped that one up to $1,500); Halbert Ellender's first book and story collec-

tion (easily two thousand), and a very rare signed copy of his Bel-Tower SF double, *Dunebuddy*, which he routinely destroyed whenever he encountered a copy (another couple of G's); and so on. Ellender was supposed to be there himself on Saturday, so I'd have to hide the display whenever he appeared.

Each of the dealers was trying to outdo the others, bringing forth rarities that hadn't been seen at any of the recent cons. Business was brisk, right from the beginning.

Margie and I set up shop on Friday morning, March 25th, using a dolly to tote the plastic boxes of priceless paperbacks from our van. We always knew in advance exactly how to arrange the books to put our best sales face forward; and we always kept a few key titles in reserve for the subsequent days of the show.

Lissa Boaz had the table across the aisle and to the left of ours. She specialized in lesbian and women writers of the 1950s through '70s. "Spade" Samuels owned the display to our right, featuring vintage mysteries, including regular- and digest magazine-sized pbs from the 1940s and '50s.

"How're you doing, Margie?" Lissa purred from her metal chair. Of course, she'd rarely deign to talk directly to *me*, a mere male.

"We're just fine," my partner said. "How about you?"

Lissa had a habit of twisting her neck back and forth whenever she was excited—all too frequently!—and then adjusting the bright pink boa that slithered around her copious bosoms and over her shoulders (she always

tended to overdress in period frippery [which Margie called "frumpery"]).

"I *found* something!" she crooned—and then held up a copy of *The Secret of Castle Dred*, the first original gothic novel published by Ace Books back in the early 1960s. It was Ace's editor, the late Donald A. Wollheim, who'd invented the package that later became the standard dress for this newly rediscovered "genre." A comely young woman was depicted fleeing in terror from an oversized house or castle lurking in the always dim background, with a single light blinking from an upper-story window.

At first Wollheim licensed various reprints of books published in the preceding decades, titles that could be warped (by a stretch of the [female] reader's imagination) into the gothic package—but soon the booming sales of the line demanded some original copy.

Of course, the notoriously tightfisted publisher, Heron Wynce, wouldn't pay a few dollars more for quality, so poor old Don, together with newly-hired editor Evelyn Grippo, was forced to turn to his usual stable of SF, mystery, and western writers (most of them men) to produce his new female-bylined gothics. One of the first of the original series was *Castle Dred*, supposedly penned by one Twilla Curtayne, a southern belle living somewhere on an old plantation in the Carolinas (ya betcha!).

Although many of the gothic novelists had eventually emerged from the literary fog that initially shrouded their mostly trite offerings, and some of the writers

were indeed of the male persuasion, occasionally with a dexter swish of the pen, Curtayne, the pioneer of the lot, had never stepped out from behind the silk curtain to reveal herself (or himself) for who—or what—she was. And she'd never penned another novel, so far as anyone knew.

"Just *what* did you find?" I asked Ms. Boaz, known in the trade as "The Boa Constrictor" for her barely legal business practices—and for her habit of wearing flamingo-hued boas.

"I've got a copy inscribed by the original author to her lover," she almost whispered, *"and it's a woman!"*

"Which," I asked, "the writer or the fan?"

"*Curtayne*, of course!" she said. "Well, I guess the other one is too, come to think of it."

I had to admit that that would *indeed* be a find, probably worthy of another grand or more to just the right buyer. Many fans had speculated on the biting, bitchy tone of Curtayne's mordant take on "Southern hospitality," and the barely disguised lesbian confrontation between her over-endowed heroine, Jezebel Langtree, and her perpetual tormentor, the equally over-the-top Madame Montragora.

"Let me see!" I said, leaning forward. She promptly rose to her feet and stepped back a pace, stashing the plastic-wrapped tome in the bowels of her oversized, alligator-encased handbag.

"No!" she hissed. "I'll only show it to the author— the *real* author! And she's going to have to pay me a pretty penny to buy this one back, let me tell you."

"Why *should* she?" I asked. "I mean, it's been more than forty years. Who really cares at this point?"

"Ohhh," Lissa said, drawing out the syllable, "I just have this little feelin', dawlin', that she'll make me an offer I just can't refuse. Ha, ha, ha—you don't know half of what *I* know."

Then she opened the first page of the book, and read the inscription: "Look sharp, Dawlin': you'll find this lurkin' beneath your covers—right along with me! Love and kisses from Your One and Own-ly—Twilla, 2/11/64."

She smirked then—I swear to God she smirked— and flounced that egregious piece of pink folderol that she always wore up around her neck and down her back, as she returned to her seat at her table.

"What was *that* all about?" Margie asked.

There wasn't much about paperbacks that Margie didn't know. She'd started as an editor at Charles N. Heckelmann's Monarch Books label in Derby, Connecticut, in the mid-1960s, and after the collapse of that line, slaved for some of the New York porn imprints of the 1960s and '70s. I'd known the woman for more than three decades, and we'd been peddling vintage paperbacks together for almost twenty years.

I told her what the "Boa Constrictor" had said.

"What a nasty piece of work that woman is," she said. "Always trying to stir things up. I can't imagine *what* she thinks she's going to accomplish."

"I think she wants to make a lot of money," I said. "It's obvious to me that she believes this signed copy

will fetch a pretty price in the right hands."

"Well, I don't imagine that the original writer would want to see it surface," Margie said. "I mean, if the poor woman were still alive, that is. She's probably long dead, you know. If it even *is* a woman."

"As if I even care," I said. I stifled a yawn.

"A *lot* of writers produced a *lot* of quickly-written crap for the sleaze and low-end paperback markets back then," my partner said. "They needed the flat-fee money to put food on their tables. There were also some major authors that got their start in that part of the business, all the way through the end of the '70s. I don't look down on them."

"I don't either, Margie," I said, "but I also can't generate a great deal of interest at this point about who wrote what. I asked Wollheim once about the author behind *Castle Dred*, and he said that the writer had really needed the money, so he was able to buy it for a $500 flat fee, and not on a royalty basis. He chortled at the memory of the sharp deal that he'd made. But he also said that, although I'd know who the writer was if he mentioned the name, he'd made a pledge never to reveal it to anyone—and he hadn't—and he wouldn't. So that was that!"

"And now Lissa thinks she knows the secret?"

"One of these days, Lissa's going to dig herself a hole that's just a wee too deep," I said, "and someone'll get angry enough to strangle her scrawny little neck with that garish scarf of hers."

Then one of our prospective customers wanted to see

the first of the Kurt Vonnegut original Gold Medals, *Canary in a Cat House*, the one with the beautiful Leo and Diane Dillon cover art, signed by the late master himself across the inside cover with a whimsical note, "My goodness! What a rarity!"

Which it certainly was! And for just a thousand cool ones, you could "share the rare" yourself!

CHAPTER TWO
"FEMALE FATAL"

Friday, March 25

"Shorty McDirk wasn't the most private of eyes, but he had a nose for nostrums, and that one talent had carried him through thick and thin and just about everything in between.

"But what to do about Glen and Glenda? There were just no easy answers. He'd tracked the terrible twins to their lair on 546th St. and Avenue Alpha, and kept a close watch on the place for 16 straight days without seeing not hide nor hair of either 'G'—before he was finally reported by the garbage men as a loiterer.

"After a rough night fending off boozers and Bolshies in the 69th Precinct clink, the private dick returned to A.A. the next morning—Day 17—and pounded on the door.

"No one answered, but the weathered slab of lemon-stained wood slowly swung open into the stifling steamy stench of an urban Hell.

> *"'Hello?' McDirk whispered as he tiptoed through the opening. Then he stumbled over the outstretched bare leg of...either Glen or Glenda!*
>
> *"'My God! It's a female fatal!' he exclaimed. "But was it really?"*

—*Female Fatal*,
by Hoggy Garfinkel (1954)

That afternoon, the show closed its exhibit area an hour early at five o'clock. Since the rooms would be locked for the night, we covered our less expensive stock with sheets, and took with us just our cash and a few small boxes of *la crème de la crème*, the latter of which we stashed temporarily in the lock box of our van. Then we drove to dinner.

Bunyan's Dive-In was a hole-in-the-wall café slathered along the south side of Division Street in "San Verdoo." It wasn't much for looks, save for the oversized, psychedelic painting of Paul and Babe plastered on the outside side wall, but the great eats trumped the rube *décor*.

You could get a huge stack of eggs, waffles, hash browns, and Polish sausages any time of the day or night, or munch on the Blue Ox Burger (three patties interlayered with bleu cheese, bacon strips, hot garlic sauce, onions, and 'shrooms), or try to scarf down the "Axe Me No Questions" triple-thick prime steak smothered with sautéed scallions, portabellas, and jalapeño peppers, or—well, you get the picture. No

one went home hungry from Bunyan's, and I wouldn't have been surprised to see ole Guy Fieri himself slumming at one of the communal benches, demonstrating his signature "hunch."

Instead, we promptly spotted a group of con attendees—the feminist book dealer, Lissa Boaz; the well-known western writer, Ferdinand Bartholomew; the "Generation XYZ" horror writer, Brody Richard "The O-Man" Dameen; the latter's new girlfriend, Gully Foyle; the nursie romance author, Kitty Gaylord; Kitty's SF writer partner, Cole Spayze—all sitting there waiting for us like a panel of self-satisfied judges.

"Well," Ferd said in his over-loud, condescending voice, "here comes one of them bookmonger folks. I guess we'll have to be careful what we say."

"That would be a first," Margie hissed in my ear, and I nearly laughed out loud.

I looked around, but the place was packed, as usual, and the only open seats were just down the row from where our "friends" were lurking.

"You want to go somewhere else?" I asked my partner.

"We're already here," she said, "and the food's pretty good. We might as well eke it out."

I ordered the "small" chickie-in-the-drink (just half the bird, fried as an entire unit in hot oil!), with smashed spuds drenched in gravy, and green beans sprinkled with slivered almonds, plus a cup of the spicy "'Fredo Soup"; and Margie picked the Chef Salad, piled high with arugula, spinach greens, lettuce, strips of ham,

chicken, beef, and turkey, several kinds of diced cheese, and a mix of chopped fresh veggies, all drizzled with a shower of the house balsamic vinaigrette. (I'd covered the place in my book with J. Howard Beeks, *Our Favorite Eats in the Inland Empire*.)

"So, Lissa," I offered, as I sipped from my kiwi iced tea and munched on the restaurant's signature Bunyan Bread (double-sized rolls) and Pterodactyl Pretzels, "have you found a buyer yet for *Castle Dred*?"

"Oh, I *do* think so!" she said, almost gushing in her enthusiasm, fiddling with the ends of the obscene boa draped around her neck. The twitching almost made it look alive.

"And just *who* is this mysterious purchaser?" I asked, not letting her off the hook.

"I told you before—*the author!*" she said. "I won't sell it to anyone else."

"You mean the writer's actually present at the show?"

"Yes, I saw her today, in fact," Lissa said, "and she was very, *very* interested. I told her that if she came to my room later this evening, we could talk business— if, that is, she wants me to keep her little secret. If she doesn't, well, then I'll offer it to someone else who's, uh, less discriminating, if you know what I mean."

"Hey, uh, I'd buy it, uh, in an instant!" The O-Man said. He was always speaking—and writing—in, uh, clichés.

"And do *what* with it?" Margie asked.

"Write, uh, a blog," he said. "I could call it, uh, 'The Writer Undead!' Or, uh, maybe, 'The Female Fatal'."

Then he chugged an entire bottle of beer.

"Isn't that supposed to be 'femme fatale'?" Margie said.

"Whatever," he said. "I don't know, uh, that many Eye-talian words."

"Have any of you actually *read* the thing?" Kitty interrupted.

"Well, *I* have, of course," Lissa said. "Or at least, I skimmed it. It's pretty bad by today's standards. I mean, old Donnie was digging pretty deep for this one. He must have been absolutely desperate for material."

"I think it was the late Evelyn Grippo running the show by that time," Margie said. "I remember meeting her at a con in the Big Apple, and hearing her talk about signing a bunch of British reprint rights for romantic suspense novels that she was going to repackage as gothics, and how she was trying to find some writers to add a few original titles to the series—but that none of the authors she'd inked thus far were really generating the atmosphere that she wanted for these books. She mentioned *Dred* in passing, but I don't recall now what she said about it. It wasn't really my thing."

"Yeah, weren't you editing those L. T. Woodward 'sex studies' for Monarch Books back then?" Kitty asked. "I thought they were penned by some sci-fi hack."

"Among other things. I was a low-level assistant in those days, so I worked on whatever Mr. Heckelmann assigned. I dealt with everything from bad SF to bad sleaze to faux Tarzan rip-offs. I sure wish, though,

I'd kept a couple of boxes each of the five Burroughs pastiches we published—I could retire now!"

"Heckelmann wrote some pretty decent oaters, as I recall," Ferd said. "Things like *River Queen* for Graphic Books."

"He also worked as a pulp magazine editor before founding Monarch Books—and after it failed, he moved on to Popular Library in the late 1960s. He knew everyone there, from Ned Pines on down, from his old pulp days, when it was still Thrilling Publications; and he was able to draw on his contacts to bring many of the same authors to his paperback lines. That's how things operated back then—still do, to a great degree. X knows Y knows Z, etc."

"Ain't it the truth," Spayze said. "But these days, there's just not much money in the business for the average Joe—except for the bestsellers, of course."

"And how many of *those* are there?" I asked. I got no reply.

"But, uh, the authors get *nothing* in, uh, return for the books you sell," Dameen said. "That, uh, just doesn't seem fair to me." He grabbed another brewski.

"No," everyone agreed.

We all knew plenty of writers who'd suddenly slipped from Easy Street to the Bowery. It could happen to any of them without warning, and the only real alternative these days was print-on-demand or e-publishing. These could bring their OP works back into press, but rarely earned anyone much in the way of hard cash. The Golden Era of paperback publishing—of print

publishing in general—was gone, and it wasn't ever coming back.

We were all gray-tinged dinosaurs, I knew, toddling off into the sunset of irrelevancy. When the dark finally came, all that would remain of any of us would be the fossilized spines of our crumbling books.

CHAPTER THREE
"I DON'T KNOW NOTHING!"

SATURDAY, MARCH 26

"Her name was Dorothy Malarkey, but it'd been a couple of years at least since she'd seen the grubby corn fields of Southeast Kansas.

"'Fess up, Malarkey,' Sergeant Brillow said, 'We know ya done the deed!'

"Then he back-slapped his hard, hairy hand right across the girl's red, rubied lips.

"'Oh! You Brutus!' she gasped, a drop of blood crawling its way right down to the cleft of her chin. 'I don't know nothing!' She thrust her twin peaks of defiance right at the police officer, twisting her body back and forth to titillate him.

"But Brillow knew better than to be swayed by the giggling of such gutterswipes. 'Ya ain't in Kansas anymore, girlie. We found the grain stashed in the vic's kitchen. It couldn't've got there by accident. And he wasn't any cook, neither.'

"'No, no, no!' she screeched, suddenly attacking the cop with her pink, inch-long fingernails. He grabbed her by the wrists, and held her fast.

"'All right! All right! I did it! He said my cornbread wasn't as good as his ma's. I just couldn't take it any more! So I put some good Wichita weed in the next batch I baked, and when he choked on that, I just laughed. Ha, ha, ha, ha, ha!'

"She was still laughing when they hauled her away to the clink."

—*Sharecropper's Girl,*
by Wiley Villemen (1960)

I awoke the next morning to a rough pounding on my door. I staggered out of bed in my underwear, wrapped myself in a robe, found my way to the exit, and greeted the new day with a not-so-joyous, *"What?!"*

Margie was standing there, a very strange look on her face. "It's...it's Lissa," she finally said. "She's dead."

"Dead?"

My brain just doesn't function well before I've filled my body with caffeine, and I simply didn't get what she was saying for a second or two.

"Dead?" I finally repeated. "How?"

"They're not saying, but there's...there's cops everywhere."

I peered over the balcony, and sure enough, several

police cars were parked near the front lobby. I knew—many folks knew—that Lissa's room, 1313, was located on the back side of the complex, well away from the traffic and noise.

"I better get dressed," I finally said. "I'll meet you in the Eatery," which was the RC's nod to a motel café.

* * * * * * *

Half an hour later I found Margie lurking at a large back booth with some authors, editors, and booksellers. The talk was all about "THE MURDER," as everyone was now calling it.

"So it's official?" I asked. "She was killed?"

"Strangled by one of her boas, they say," Levi Barton said next to me. "You know, she had it coming!"

"That's a bit gauche," Kitty Gaylord said. "After all, the woman's barely in her coffin."

"She's not in *any* coffin," Barton said. "If they've removed the body, she's down at the morgue waiting to be cut open from hat to twat."

"How disgusting!" Margie said. "Why do you always have to be so vile, Levi?"

"Well, let's face it," he said, "no one much cared for the bitch. And she *was* a bitch, no question."

We might have all privately agreed with him, but none of us cared for the blunt, insensitive way with which he handled the passing of a colleague.

"Enough of that," I said. "Do they have any suspects?"

"I hear the cops are questioning everyone, but I don't think they have anybody particular in mind—at least

not yet," Kitty said.

"What about the expo?" Margie asked.

"They haven't made a decision," Kitty said. "Tomás is talking it over with several of the other organizers, and they'll have an announcement by noon. Everything's shut down until then."

"But, surely they can't go on…," Margie said.

* * * * * * *

But they *would* go on, or at least that's what the flyer that was handed out a half-hour later said. The second session would open at one, and continue until six that evening, and the third would take place tomorrow at the usual time.

Meanwhile, the police had finally located the Eatery (superior detective work, that!), and were systematically asking the patrons if they'd known the deceased, and in what capacity, where they'd been last evening between the hours of nine and ten P.M., and if they knew of any reason why someone would want to kill Melissa (which turned out to be her *real* name—who knew?).

"I'm surprised she lasted this long," Barton said in such a loud voice that *all* heard his outburst. "She was just a nasty, nasty, *nasty* individual that everyone purely hated. She had it coming, if anyone did!"

"It was that *book*!" Kitty said, "That *Castle Dred* thing. That's what got her killed!"

"You think the author murdered her?" I asked.

"Who else?" she said. "I heard the police didn't find

it in her room."

"Every dealer here had a motive," I said, "a big financial one."

"Yes, but who'd buy it now?" Barton asked. "The seller would immediately be suspect."

"Not if it were sold 'under the table,' so to speak," Margie said. "If the author's really here at the con, then she or he would want to stop the secret from getting out."

"Just what I stated," Kitty said. "It was the *writer*, no question."

"Excuse me. Were you folks at the convention?" someone asked us from behind.

I turned and looked up at a nondescript man in a black suit and tie. He flashed a badge at us. "Lieutenant Alwin Pfisch, S.V.P.D. Homicide," he said. "I'd like to talk with each of you separately, before you return to the show this afternoon. We've set up in Room 1003 in the motel for interviews. Sergeant Hamm"—he nodded to the police officer lurking a few steps back— "will take your names and contact info. Thank you."

"But I don't know nothing!" Kitty said.

"Nonetheless," Pfisch said, "You'll each please make yourselves available for a brief interview."

Then he left to accost some other patrons, but the Sergeant remained to record the particulars from everyone at the table. When he departed, trailing in his supervisor's wake, we all just looked at each other. I think everyone was thinking the same thing: "Was that a killer sitting across from me?"

CHAPTER FOUR
"YOU NAME UH?"

SATURDAY, MARCH 26

"'You name Uh?' asked Mr. Fan, the well-known detective from Koreatown.

"'Yeah,' I growled, scowling up at the dumb copper. 'Ima Uh.'

"'You a Uh?' Fan said, squinting down at me.

"'No,' I said. 'I'm Uh! Ima Uh!' I thrust my plenteous bosoms up at his face, wriggling them like overripe cantaloupes. 'See!'

"'What I said!' Fan dangoed, jumping back from my dangerous dodos. 'You kill Hu!'

"'Hu?' I said. 'Uh, Hu did I kill?'

"'Hu, Uh,' came the reply.

"I knew I was in a manure pile of trouble. This was beginning to look a lot like a Japanese puzzle box, and unless I moved those wooden slats back and forth in just the right way, I'd never crack this case wide open. And

then Hu would Fan arrest but Uh—a damaged
dame like me?"

—*Insclutable Puzzle Box*,
by Cosmo d'Ombre (1948)

"Let's see, uh, you name, uh…," Pfisch said, paging through several lists of names. "I know I've got it here somewhere."

I finally told him who I was, or we would have been sitting there for the rest of the day.

"Oh, yes, here you are"—which I thought was pretty obvious myself. "Where were you after nine o'clock last night?"

"In my room, of course," I said. "I was reading a book."

"A *book*? You fellas actually *read* some of these things?"

"Only the cheap ones, Lieutenant. The expensive items, we sell!"

"Of course. Can anyone vouch for your presence there at that time?"

"No," I said. "I tend to read alone."

"I hear you were involved in an altercation with Ms. Boaz yesterday."

I shook my head in an emphatic "No."

"We all argued with Lissa, most of the time," I said. "She wasn't the kind of person who gave you the warm and fuzzies, if you know what I mean." And then I told him about the book.

"You *really* think she was killed over an old paper-

back?" the policeman asked. "I mean, that sounds a bit far-fetched to me."

"I heard a story once," I said. "I don't know if it's true, but I believed it, and so do most of the dealers I know.

"There was a collector named Franky Froggo or something like that—not his real name, of course, but the persona he adopted in public. He was trying to put together a complete mint set of the Dell 10¢ paperbacks—half-sized productions of sixty-four pages, each one stapled through the spine. They did something like thirty-six of them in 1951, including works by major writers that never appeared in that format again. They're very pricey, particularly the unread copies—and assembling a good-quality run of the books is nigh unto impossible these days.

"Well, supposedly he was attending a con in St. Louis, and he and a dealer named Cory Felice happened upon the display at Freddie the Cur's table at the same time, coming from opposite ends, see; and they reached the collision point just where the best stuff was housed under glass. And there was the Robert A. Heinlein ten-center, *Universe*, beckoning to both of them simultaneously.

"Felice knew that he could resell the book for a significant mark-up back in the Big Apple—and poor old Froggo knew that *that* particular item was just what he needed to complete his set. They both shouted 'It's mine!' at the same time to dear Freddie, who *really* had them by the short hairs: he could start a bidding

war, and who knows where it would end!

"But when Froggo saw who his competition was, he realized immediately that he couldn't outbid Felice. So he calmly reached into the backpack he always carried with him, pulled out a petite revolver, and shot him full of holes. Then he politely asked the Cur for his book.

"Freddie assures me this actually happened. So yes, Lieutenant, I do believe that people will kill over such things, particularly when reputations are at stake. Whoever the author is, she's never been willing to emerge from the dark shadows of her past. I don't think she wants to now, either."

That was the end of our first interview—but it wasn't the last.

CHAPTER FIVE
"I'LL MAKE YOU COME TO MAMA!"

SATURDAY, MARCH 26

"Madame Montragora watched with bright-dark eyes as Filly and Taisy tied the beauteous girl to the old tanning table, hooking each arm and leg to halters that spread her body wide and open. Jezzy was sobbing in terror, begging for a mercy that she knew would never arrive.

"'Please,' she said. 'Oh, please. I'll do anything you want.'

"'Yes, you will,' the mistress of the house stated. 'Strip her!' she ordered her servants.

"'But, Ma'am, she's...she's one of the gentry,' Filly said.

"'Strip her, I say! Slash every last linen and shift from her Satan-infested body. She must be taught a lesson!

"'I'll make you come to Mama!' she told the wretchedly overendowed governess."

After grabbing a bite at The Brer Bunny, which featured Samothracian cuisine, Margie and I opened for business once more that afternoon; but the crowds were small, much less than the day before, and the entire atmosphere seemed very subdued.

"Damn and blast!" I said. "It's just not fair. We spend the entire year getting ready for this event, and it's being ruined by someone pursuing a private vendetta. I mean, it's like a bad paperback novel."

"You don't know that," she said. "Maybe Lissa threatened the writer with exposure, when she couldn't pay the price she was asking. Somebody like Freddie the Cur could outbid anyone if he saw a buck to be made down the line. You know that."

"Yeah, but…like I said, it's not fair that we're the ones being made to pay the piper here—*all of us*. Not right at all."

"I'm not disagreeing with you," she said, "I'm really not. But there's nothing we can do about it until the cops catch the killer."

She rose from her seat and turned to help someone whom I couldn't see, but then I had a customer too, so we finally sold a few books. We had a long way to go, though, just to break even.

Then I saw the lanky form of Lieutenant Pfisch approaching, and I whispered, "Here comes da fuzz!"—to which Margie said, "Stop that!"

He halted in front of our table, and said: "You

know, I was thinking about what you said last night, and I thought I'd better take a look at that novel you mentioned. You know, *Castle*, uh...."

"*Castle Dred*," I said. "I think we've got one or two somewhere. Not a prime copy, you understand: 'spine intact, but some creases,' as Vanis Victoroff would say."

"I just want to read it to see if anything there gives me an idea or two."

"Margie! You know where that book went?" I was plowing through the Ace "K" series, looking for the worn copy of K-99 that I knew we had in stock.

"Here it is!" she said, holding up the item I was seeking.

"What's it doing over *there*?" I asked. "Somebody must have moved it while pawing through our table. Here you go, Lieutenant—it's on the house!"

"No, sir, I can't do that, thank you just the same," the policeman said. "I'll pay my way with the legal tender of the land. Let me give me the total, please."

I charged him ten bucks, which was a fair price, considering the less-than-ideal condition of the volume. But the pages were intact, so he could read to his heart's delight.

Oh, I remembered *Castle Dred*, all right; I recalled the plot very well indeed, since it was so over-the-top.

Jezebel Langtree's father is left penniless in the aftermath of the Civil War, when his massive investment in Confederate War Bonds suddenly turns into worthless paper. Jezzy, the twenty-two-year-old eldest

child, whose beau had been killed in the Pickett line at Gettysburg, is forced to take a job as governess to the children of the House of Montragora, located a few miles outside the small county seat of Georgeville, Virginia.

Col. Phibeas Montragora had maintained his fortune by selling horses, food, and stock to both sides in the War Between the States, and now has become the largest land owner in Rapunzel County, buying estates cheaply as the proprietors default on their loans. He has his greedy eyes firmly fixed on Hilldale, the Langtree farm, which lies astride a major highway into the new state of West Virginia. He wants to build an, uh, special "inn" there for the weary business travelers that he knows are coming.

Madame Lucrezia Montragora runs her household like a petty tyrant, insisting on having her way in everything; and her two young daughters, Hannabelle and Sarralee, follow their mother's lead. Jezzy's life at Montragore House becomes a living hell, a game of bait-and-switch that she can never win. And yet she has no choice but to continue: her regular income, small as it is, is the only thing that is keeping her family solvent.

But there's something very strange about the Montragoras, Jezzy discovers, something that they're hiding from the outside world. Other than the old patriarch, who's always away on business somewhere, the mansion contains no men—all of the servants, all of the near relations, are female.

One day she uncovers the family Bible, with its

record of births, deaths, and marriages; and finds, much to her surprise, that it does include the names of numerous male offspring, but that none of them ever seem to carry on the line. Indeed, most die soon after reaching the age of fourteen or fifteen. And then comes the greatest shock of all: the marriage record of Lucrezia Montragora with Phibeas Van Damm! He's not a Montragora by blood!

When Madame Montragora enters the room and discovers Jezzy holding the book, she yells to the servants for help, and before the governess can do anything to save herself, has her tied and bound in a subterranean room deep beneath the old structure. Then she strips away the young woman's clothes, and begins a very strange torture session, caressing her with feathered boas. "I'll make you come to Mama!" she says. "You'll confess everything before you're through!"

All seems lost until the Colonel returns from his latest venture, and frees Jezzy from her bonds, wrapping her in his great-cloak. As she flees from the mansion in the night, she can hear the two adults shouting at each other—and then she sees the flames spitting from the windows, as Montragore House finally meets its ugly fate, taking with it the perverted women who've inhabited its walls.

I could see why there'd never been a sequel.

CHAPTER SIX

"HOW'S IT HANGIN'?"

SATURDAY, MARCH 26

"Jackson rode into town on his albino palomino, settin' high in the saddle and looking for b'ar.

"He drew his six-shooter and fired a shot straight up at the sky—and then heard it plunk right down again, through the top of the tin water tower, the one with Alab-ster whitewashed across the pale, faded top of the tank. Water began drippin' out the bottom.

"Several townsfolk wandered out onto the dusty main street of Alabaster, Kansas (not far from Dodge City), but only one person really welcomed him—Mr. Josiah Murdo, the mortician.

" 'How's it hangin'?' the embalmer asked. Jackson was always good for business.

" 'Got me a wanted poster for One-Eye Dick,' the gunman said, whippin' it out and wavin' it

'round and 'round in the bright noonday sun. 'They said he was lurkin' here somewheres.'

"'Seen him down in the saloon jus' this mornin',' Murdo said. 'Looked to be sailin' at half-mast.'

"'He'll be all-busted-up by the time I'm through with him,' Jackson said. Just then the doors of the Lucky Gal slammed open, and Dick himself came wobblin' out, ramblin' back and forth while he tried to pull himself together.

"'I sees you, Dick,' Jackson said, hoppin' down from his paley pony. He wiped his hands on his flannel shirt, and unbuttoned the straps over his guns. 'Prepare to die, you dog!' he shouted.

"But Dick was already pullin' out his massive weapon, and levelin' it right at the bounty hunter's heart. 'Gotcha!' he said.

"Jackson did a tumbly to his left, yankin' out his one-eyed monster at the same time, and firin' from a prone position right behind the water trough that his palomino was sippin' from. One-Eye Dick's shot plonked a hole in the wood next to his head—but Jackson's didn't miss his target.

"'Too bad!' he yelled, as his opponent dropped dead-first into the dust. 'Ya had a big one, all right, but ya jus' couldn't get it in play, could ya?

"Now, that's a truth that every gunslinger knows: the bigger they are, the harder they fall."

—*Not Far from Dodge City*,
by Brody Dameen (1959)

The horror writer Brody Richard Dameen was about fifty-five years of age, but he looked at least eighty, as he staggered over to signing area "D" at three o'clock, a couple of tables down from ours. He'd obviously been sipping the breakfast of champions again—bourbon *sans* the rocks.

Dameen had started his career writing westerns for Star Books and porn for Bee-Line, and then had tried spy spoofs in the 1960s, and moved to horror in the '70s. His one big claim to fame was the bestselling paperback, *The O-Man* (Pinochle Books), the tale of a demon-fighting action hero infused with not-so-delicate shades of both James Bond and *The Exorcist*, which had spawned twenty-seven really bad sequels, and an equally popular yet despicable motion picture starring a very young Brucie Campo (plus a dozen slimy straight-to-video offspring).

Of late, however, "The O-Man," as he was fond of calling himself, had fallen on hard times, and was now reduced to peddling his memoirs, *Five Decades of Pornorror*, and endless analyses of how his better-selling competitors had ripped him off.

The line of fans waiting patiently to receive his precious signature was not nearly as long as that for

the next writer, Van Cott, who was hovering above one of his books, trying to remember what his name was.

I asked Margie to watch our table, and moseyed on over. "How's it hangin', Brody?" I asked.

He grimaced a bit, and then sipped from the pink straw sticking through the top of the plastic cup in front of him. "Man, it's, uh, tough out there today," he said, "but things're, uh, looking up. I've got a deal working that should, uh, should, uh…."

He shook his head to clear out the cobwebs, but it obviously didn't work this time, so he said again, "It should, uh, really…."

"Yeah, I understand," I said. "When you're done, Brody, could you sign the copies we have of your books?"

"Sure, man, anything for a friend. Hey, when I'm, uh, back on Park Place again, I'm going to, uh, to—I'll remember the people who, uh, helped me, you know?"

"Yeah," I said. "I'll count on it."

I was shaking my head when I sat down again.

"Still in bad shape?" Margie asked.

"Worse than ever. Now he says he's got a deal going."

"He's been saying that for the last decade."

I'd just sold a copy of a mint-condition Pony Book from the postwar period when I saw Lieutenant Pfisch and Sergeant Hamm coming our way.

"They're baaack!" I hissed at my partner, nodding down the aisle.

"I wonder what they want," she said.

"Ms. Brittleback," the Lieutenant said, "I wonder

if we could have a word with you again. In private, please."

"What's this all about?" I asked.

"We have some more questions for her," Hamm said.

"About what?"

"I think that's a matter of police business," Pfisch said. "Will you come with us, please?" he added, nodding at Margie.

"What should I do?" she asked, turning to me, fear etched in her eyes.

The room around us had gotten very quiet all of a sudden.

"Are you charging her with anything, Lieutenant?" I asked.

"Not at this time," he said.

"And if she refuses?"

"I wouldn't recommend that," the policeman said. "You see, sir, we have a witness who can place her outside Ms. Boaz's room at nine o'clock last night. We want to know what she was doing there!"

CHAPTER SEVEN
"YOU DON'T UNDERSTAND"

SATURDAY, MARCH 26

"'You don't understand, Jesse, you just don't,' Laura gushed, reaching one lovely, lanky hand 'south of the border.' 'A girl has her needs, too!'

"'But I promised Father Fritto that I'd keep myself pure,' her boyfriend said, 'that I'd drink only distilled water and eat unleavened bread, and abstain from the, uh, baser acts of life, until, until....'

"'Until what, my love?' she asked, panting to keep her rubbed-raw emotions in cheek. She was a sprightly girl raised on goat's milk and chocolate balls, and she had a Pollyanna's picture of life in the Big Palooza. Still, she'd kept her goal firmly planted in front of her eyes—and she wanted it now!

"'Until I found "urbvana,"' he said, 'Father Fritto's life-freeing, formal "D" hybrid.' He

showed her the elongated bulb of the carefully cultivated plant.

"'But I can give you something more!' Laura exclaimed, smiling her cheery, toothy grin at him.

"'What?' Jesse asked, leaning towards her expectantly.

"'Silly boy!' she said, grasping both her lover's root—and his prompt attention. 'Nervana!'

"'Ohm, my God!'"

—*Urban Commune Nurse*,
by Kitty Gaylord (1963)

Margie returned ninety minutes later. She looked shaken and drawn—and more than a little distracted.

"What did they want to know?" I asked her, when she'd settled in her seat.

"Uh, what?" she whispered, head cast down.

"The police," I said.

"Well, someone claimed to have seen me in front of Lissa's door a little after nine o'clock last night."

"Who?" I asked.

"They wouldn't say." My partner's head continued to droop, and I could barely hear her mumbles over the conversations behind me.

"And *were* you there?"

"Yes," she said.

"Why, Margie? *Why?*"

I was really getting concerned now. Maybe she

needed an attorney.

"I…you don't understand. You…you just don't." She was back to whispering again.

"Try me," I said.

"I wanted to save an old friend's reputation, that's all. I wanted to talk some sense into Lissa. But when I got to her room, the door was cracked open; I went inside and saw her lying there dead, with the book already gone. I found a small corner of the cover grasped between her fingers, and I took it from her. Whoever killed her had literally snatched it from her dying hand.

"That's what I told the cops. I don't know why they didn't arrest me—I can't prove any of it."

"*What* friend?" I asked. "*What* reputation?"

"That was *my* copy of *Castle Dred.* It was inscribed to *me,* OK? I knew the writer almost fifty years ago, during my last year of high school, just before I came to New York. We were…well, we were close. I wound up writing some of those gothics too, as well as porn books and other stuff, in the mid-1960s and '70s. But I *didn't* write *Dred*—my best friend did. We had a kind of contest going, over which of us would get published first—and she won!" A streak of tears furrowed down both sides of her face.

"But she never came to the Big Apple, like me. I urged her to join me, I really did; I told her that she could find acceptance there, that she had talent to spare, but she was afraid to leave her family. Instead, she married a local banker and had a couple of kids, and…I don't really know what. She got divorced and

moved away from that small town, finally, and I lost track of her decades ago. I don't know what became of her. I didn't have any family left myself, so I never went back—didn't *want* to go back."

"But who *was* she?"

"Just a sweet girl whose head was filled with dreams—like mine. We loved literature, we loved the great authors, we wanted to become just like them. Elizabeth Barrett Browning, the Beats, everything old and new excited us. We were young then: we thought all things were possible. They weren't! She didn't have the gumption to take it to the next step. I did, although I never amounted to much as a writer. I was just a hack. Turned out my talent—and hers—didn't measure up, really. So, maybe she was wiser than me, I don't know."

"Was Lissa right in saying that she's here at the con?"

"How would I know?" Margie said. "I haven't seen or talked to her since 1964. I don't know if I'd even recognize her now. We were both twenty back then, so she'd be about sixty-six or –seven if she were still alive. And what difference does it make anyway? I lost track of my copy years ago, during one of my frequent moves. I probably traded the book for something else to read, or gave it to a friend."

"Well, it obviously made a difference to someone— enough of a difference to kill for," I said.

"If she had a position in society, she might have been concerned about having it compromised."

"In this day and age?" I said. "Who cares anymore whether you're straight or gay?"

"A *lot* of people care, particularly in business and professional circles, *particularly* in small towns," my partner said. "That's why I went to see Lissa. I thought I could buy the book back for the business, and just write it off *my* account. I thought I could take care of the problem once and for all. If my friend wanted her pen name kept secret, I could at least do that much for her. But...."

I sighed. "What *was* her name?" I finally asked.

"That's my business, OK?"

"Did you tell the cops all this?"

"Of course."

"Did you tell them her name?"

"Yes."

"Then why not me?"

She looked up at me then, and after a long pause, said: "I don't think I really want you to know."

CHAPTER EIGHT
"I DON'T KNOW WHY"

SATURDAY, MARCH 26

"The Sundogger *came roaring out of the nebula, zap guns blazing at both ends.*

"'Bzzzt, bzzzt,' they went, as they chewed through the hull of the Kymkurdashianan battleship.

"'Burka, burka,' the alien vessel responded, sending a stream of supercharged x-beams back the other direction.

"'They're outgunned! Why don't they surrender?' Sergeant Mazeltoff yelled over the steam jetting into the control room. He wiped the sweat from his overheated brow.

"'I don't know why,' I shouted back at him, adjusting the valve to inject more super-coal into the engine. Trying to predict what a Kymkurdashian might do was almost impossible, since they acted only from irrational premises. They built beautiful hulls, no question, but their control-and-command functions were mostly

lacking—and that made them very dangerous foes indeed.

" 'They're a-comin' right at us!' Scottie the Res-geek said in an even tone of voice. Only an insufficiency of test-tubes ever bothered him.

" 'Then blast the buggers!' I ordered. I pressed the big red button on the console.

"The resulting 'Boom!' rattled the whole ship. I glanced out the porthole. A giant brown projectile was hurtling right towards the on-coming enemy cruiser. It spattered over their space-wind shield, rendering them effectively blind.

" 'Right turn! Right turn!' I told the helms-lady, and she grabbed the great wheel and ro-tated it ninety degrees. The Sundogger *slid just under the alien ship. We all turned to watch the alien metal cylinder plow a furrow into the third planet of Rastus.*

" 'Gee! That was close!' Scottie mumbled.

" 'Yeah,' I said, 'but I never had any doubts when I saw that turd from the sun!' "

—*Third from the Sun,*
by Cole Spayze (1957)

My conversation with Margie had left me very unsettled, and I spent the rest of the afternoon in a semi-daze. We'd never had a romantic relationship—I mean, I understood that much about her from the beginning—but we had been close friends for a great

many years, and I thought I knew all of the important things that there were to know about her. Obviously, I was wrong.

I couldn't possibly imagine Margie as the killer—she was just too down-to-earth, it seemed to me. I didn't think she had the willingness to kill that seems innate in certain individuals, although I knew that almost anyone could be pushed to murder under the right circumstances. But she was one of those individuals whom I regarded as solid and practical and not likely to allow herself to be upset in the kind of way that I envisioned killers to be. But I'd been wrong before, and there was much about her that I clearly didn't understand.

What I did know was this: Margie had just become the prime suspect for the murder of Lissa Boaz, at least from the point of view of the cops. I assumed that they had her prints in Lissa's room, in addition to the supposed eyewitness account of her visitation there at the right time of the evening. I wouldn't think that a boa would retain prints, but these days, with the technology that the cops have available, there could be a DNA residue or something like that—although those kinds of tests took longer than overnight to gain results, I knew.

The problem was this: in order to disprove Margie's connection with the murder, I had to find the real killer, and do so in a way that that individual's guilt was established beyond any doubt. But there were any number of possible murderers available. Paperback mongering

had become a cutthroat business in the past decade. I knew all of the vendors at the show, if not in person, at least by reputation; and perhaps a third of them had been accused or suspected, at one time or another, of questionable business practices. It's not much of a jump to go from cheating someone (semi-legalized robbery) to banging them over the head to steal their property, which is what might be involved here.

And then there were the possible personal motivations. What if Margie's former "friend" was indeed present at the proceedings, perhaps greatly aged or disguised in some way, having been tipped off by Lissa that the one thing that might identify her after all these decades was about to be revealed? This seemed far-fetched to me, because I still couldn't imagine why anyone would actually care about something that had occurred a half-century earlier; but people do strange things sometimes, and reputation, status, and position mean just about everything to certain kinds of individuals. So it was a possible motive—just barely, in my estimation.

Also, Lissa was not, shall we say, well-liked. She had an acerbic, biting personality that rubbed many people (including myself) the wrong way. She gave feminism and lesbianism a very bad name. She enjoyed deliberately doing things that punished or hurt other people, for reasons that only made sense to her. So, she might have been killed by one of her myriad enemies, from both inside and outside the business.

The only thing that I could think to do that might

eventually lead me to the murderer was to track the book. *What* had happened to the inscribed copy of *The Secret of Castle Dred*? According to the rumor mill, the police hadn't located it in her room. Someone—the killer or an onlooker—had walked away with it. Someone had it now. They wouldn't be able to sell it openly, not with the notoriety that had now been attached to it; but there would be a buyer, sooner or later, who would agree to purchase it under the counter. I knew this business, and I knew that lack of scruples went both ways.

"Have you thought about getting an attorney?" I asked Margie.

"I have a friend who's a lawyer," she said. "I phoned him an hour ago. He recommended a good criminal practitioner, but I'm hoping it won't come to that."

"Unless they find someone better, I think you'll almost certainly be arrested," I said. "You need to be prepared for that possibility."

She sighed. "I don't know why I went to Lissa's room last night, I really don't. In retrospect, it seems so damned stupid. I know what kind of person Lissa is. She'd only have been interested in hard cash, cash on the line, and I don't bring very much to these shows. She had to have someone—or someones—on her string, or she never would have brought the book with her. She *knew* an interested party would be here. But *who*?"

"You're sure it wasn't your friend?"

"How would I recognize her? I haven't seen anyone

here that reminded me of her—not even close. But it's been so long. She's never made any effort down the decades to contact me, and on the one occasion when I went back home in the late '60s, she refused to meet me—I think she was afraid that her husband would realize that our friendship was more than that. A few years later, when I returned for my Mom's funeral, she was gone—no one knew where. My brother had left town not long after I did for the city lights, and there was no one still close to me that I could ask. Someone told me later that she'd left her husband and remarried—but they had no contact information. I have no idea even what her name might be now—or if she's still alive."

"OK," I said, "so let's assume Lissa knew what she was doing. She may have been a real shit, but she always made a profit. She must have had at least two possible bidders for the book who'd agreed to come here. They could have been dealers themselves, or 'interested parties,' or both. How would she have handled it?"

Margie thought for a moment. "Well, *I* think she would have called both of them, told them what she had, and said that she was initially going to conduct a private auction; and then, if the bids were insufficient, she would have told them that she'd go public, and try to sell it that way. She might have given them a window between, say, seven and nine P.M., and made appointments for specific times for each of the interested parties—with the most interested individual being left for last. And then she'd try to jack up the price while

reaming them out with the threat of revelation."

"And if that final potential purchaser couldn't match the price…?"

"Maybe they slipped over the edge—and killed her."

"Makes sense," I said. "Now all we have to do is find the culprit!"

CHAPTER NINE
"HE WAS NEVER A FRIEND TO ANYONE"

SATURDAY, MARCH 26

"I turned the corner at Orzechówka Street, and crept like a rat between the shadows, watching for any movement up ahead, my hand firmly clasped around my strzelbą dwururka. You could have cut the smog with a stainless steel carving knife—but at least the damp air muffled the passage of my iron-toed leather boots. Swish, swish, swish they went, as I moved slowly and carefully from doorway to doorway, waiting for the bullet that never came.

"We were two hunters stalking our prey—one another—with an intensity that belied the coldness of the silent war we fought—just two hunters bent upon the destruction of the living symbol of a political system, one red, the other red, white, and blue. Which swatch would survive unstitched remained to be seen.

"'Blat,' I heard, and instinctively ducked—not that it would have done me much good—as a chip of pink brick scoured a furrow up one cheek. I wiped the blood away.

"'Not quite "Gut Enuff," Comrade!' I chirped into the night, zipping a taut little package right back at my enemy. His name was Colonel Żyleniec, but I called him Żylak, or 'Varicose Vein,' which I knew infuriated him. We'd played this game many times before over the past two decades, sometimes on my turf, and now on his. But I had a feeling that this would be our last bout upon the chessboard of life.

"'You von't escape me this time!' he yelled back, sending another bullet my way. 'Blat,' 'blip,' 'blink' went our mini-missiles hurling back and forth, forth and back. Finally, I could stand the strain no more, and I stepped out in the middle of the street, right where the trolley tracks cut their twin furrows through the cobblestones—and Żylak followed suit. We would finally resolve our issues like the iron-nosed men we were.

"We fired simultaneously, but I think my second barrel must have tipped the balance, for the Polish Colonel slumped down on his knees to the wet pavement, staining his one good western suit, and dropping his fuming fuzja right there on the bricks.

" 'I die,' he said, coughing up gouts of pink-hinged blood (still a diehard Commie). 'I die, but you and I, ve vere the same! The same to the very end!'

" 'No,' I said out loud, 'we were never the same, Comrade.'

"You see, I was a friend to mankind and my dog; but that Żylak, he was never a friend to anyone!"

—Incident at Czyścimnie,
by Donnie Grollman Opdyke (1967)

We finally shooed away the last lookie-loo of the afternoon, packed up the primo pbs and covered the rest with a cloth, and got out just as Tomás and the security guards were locking up the place. We were both exhausted, for more reasons than one. I saw what appeared to be a plainclothes policeman watching us as we headed towards our van.

I locked the carton of quality books in the safe box in the vehicle, and then we drove the few blocks to Restaurant Row on the other side of the freeway. I suggested the Jade Tiger, the best Chinese restaurant in town, and Margie just nodded—I don't think she really cared at that point.

I ordered some hot-and-sour soup and a platter of Shanghai dumplings, and we munched away in silence—or at least I did—while contemplating the day's events.

"I just can't believe she's gone," Margie finally said.

"You mean Lissa?"

"She may have been a nasty piece of work, but she was alive, you know what I mean? The bristles were real. She didn't deserve to die—not over some fading pages slapped between cheap cover art. I mean, Ace never spent that much money on *anything*. My friend was paid just $500 for *Castle Dred*. Of course, she was only nineteen at the time."

"I remember Don Wollheim telling me once how he had to scrimp on everything, while his boss lived in this grandiose place out on Long Island. But why did he publish *that* book?" I said. "I mean, it was pretty bad, even by Ace's standards."

"Yeah, it was no classic, that's for sure," Margie said, "although at the time, we both thought it was a real lark. Like mine, her novel satirized some of the 'in' people in town. I had the impression that she knew somebody who worked for the company, and Wollheim was ordered to buy it by someone further up the chain."

"Really! That's very interesting."

"It is, but like so much of this, it's old history. Who cares now?"

"Somebody cares, that's for sure," I said. "Somebody cares a great deal. Did your friend come from a prominent family?"

"I always thought so," she said. "She lived in a big house just outside of town, and they always drove the newest cars, and went on vacations to exotic places. But now that I think about it, I don't really know what her father did. He was away a lot, and I rarely saw him

in person. She never talked about him much; I had the impression they weren't very close. He was a banker or real estate investor or something like that—maybe. She married one of his friends, someone much older. She wasn't too happy about it, but she told me at the time that she had no choice, that if she came to New York to live, her father would find her and drag her back again."

"How utterly medieval," I said. "I mean, you can't do things like that these days."

"Back then, in a small town, if you were connected—yes, you could, and everyone in authority would back you up too."

Then I heard a loud voice raised in anger, and I looked over at the high booth across the room from us. Brody Dameen was arguing with someone sitting back in the shadows. Suddenly, his opposite number leaned forward into the light, and I recognized the fat face of Freddie the Cur, as he stuffed another wonton into his mouth.

Freddie was a big man in every sense of the word: tall and long and round and ugly, like the girl from Ipanema blown inside out. He must have weighed at least three hundred pounds, but you could section that lard piece by piece, if you dared, and never find a heart. If he'd ever had one, he'd fried it in grease and eaten it a long time ago.

"Don't you threaten me, you tipsy little turd!" I heard him tell the "O-Man." "I'll crush you like the bug you are."

"But I have it!" Dameen said, and then dropped his voice, and I couldn't make out anything else that they said to each other, except, *"I do!"*

"What was *that* all about?" Margie asked.

But before I could respond, Gully Foyle, Brody's "significant other," stormed into the room, and halted right in front of the two men. She was a blonde woman of perhaps forty, well-dressed and well-apportioned, if you know what I mean.

"What are *you* doing here, Freddie?" she hissed—just loud enough so we could hear. "Leave him alone. He never did anything to you."

"But, I…uh, I…," Brody said.

"And *you*! What's the matter with you, dealing with the likes of him? You know what kind of person he is."

"But…."

"Come with me, now, Dearie. It's time we got back to our room. *Iron Chef*'ll be on soon, and I know you like that." Then she looked at the book dealer again, and almost spit at him. "*You* can pick up the tab, you asshole!"

She eased Dameen out of the booth, and carefully supported him as he wobbled from the room, dragging our eyes with them.

But when I looked back across the restaurant, all I saw were the beady little orbs of Freddie the Cur staring right at me. He stuck out his pasty slug of a tongue, and wiped his bottom lip with it, left to right, like a dog cleaning his chops. He might as well have shouted to the patrons, "I *see* you, *old friend*, and we'll

take care of business later."

Yet he was never a friend to anyone, not even to himself.

CHAPTER TEN
"GOODBYE! GOOD LUCK!"

Saturday, March 26

"What can you say about a fifty-four-year-old girl who died?

"Septuagenarian bestselling writer Julius Manderley sat upright on his horse, Daisy Bell, the very beast who'd kicked his beloved to death after she'd tried to force just one more beet into her spayed jaws, while he pondered the strange vicissitudes of life.

"Theirs had been a whirlwind, twenty-four-day romance, beginning at his hospital bed, where he'd been recovering from near-fatal biblio-spasms to his fingers and arms. Writhing in agony, unable to find relief, he suddenly discovered his pain-wracked wrist being massaged by the twinkling toes of the overendowed Nurse Judi Bell, and was immediately captivated.

"Then followed a gusto of events that he could scarcely recall to mind, being somewhat

alzheimeristically compromised—of moto-cross excursions into the Oregon mountains, of long rides on Daisy Bell and Tinkle Bell on the still longer, dusty trails to nowhere, of moonlit nights trying to find their way back home again—always with his beloved Judi Bell at his side, massaging him with those ter-rific toenails!

"Ah, such ecstasy!

"But all things do finally peter out, and when the veginarian Judi Bell tried to 'beet' poor Daisy Bell one time too many, the placid palomino turned on her owner, and kicked her kaput with one mighty blow.

"And now—poor Julius was left all alone once again, with just his fractured memories and his meaningless millions to keep him com-pany—although he did still have the undying love of his two horsies!

"'Love means never having to say you're hoary,' he said to no one in particular. 'Good-bye! Good luck!'"

—*Love, Love, Love!*
by Hyacinth Peppercorn (1963)

Lieutenant Pfisch was waiting for us back at the motel, with several men in blue, and informed Margie that she was under arrest for the murder of Lissa Boaz. "Or should I say 'Margaret Storm,' Ms. Brittleback?" he said. "Turns out you have a record under that name.

Why am I not surprised that you told me nothing about this in our little interview this afternoon?"

"You didn't ask," she said.

"What record?" I asked.

"She was convicted of dealing drugs in New York back in the 1970s," Pfisch said. "Served a year, too, before being released on good behavior."

"It was all a mistake," she said, shaking her head. "And I *wasn't* dealing. I just bought some pot for my own use."

"That's what they all say. You can explain that to the judge when the time comes."

Then he read her her rights and handcuffed her. Margie turned to me and said: "Call my attorney! His number's 909-555-2212. Leave a message. I'll be at...." She looked at the Lieutenant.

Pfisch told me where they were taking her.

"Find the real killer! That's the *only* thing you can do to help."

Then they hauled her across the lot to the police car, stuffed her in the back seat, and drove away.

I was stunned by the turn of events, although I'd been half-expecting this. I couldn't decide what to do. Then I thought about the conversation that we'd over-heard in the restaurant—and what Brody had told me earlier in the day—and I decided that I needed to see the "O-Man" one more time.

I phoned the attorney that Margie had mentioned, and then later headed for the motel. Brody and Gully were staying on the back side of the Royal Crest, in

Room 1333. I took the elevator to the thirteenth floor, went out to the external balcony that fronted on all of the rooms, and had to walk almost to the end of the row.

I pounded on their door until Gully finally cracked it open.

"What do you want?" she asked. I could barely hear her.

"I need to talk to Brody," I said.

"He's sick."

"He's drunk," I said, "but that's nothing new. I still need to talk to him. Or would you rather that I told the cops about the little scene that I witnessed at the Jade Tiger a few hours ago."

"No, don't do that!" she said. "All right, but keep it short, OK?"

Brody was propped up in front of the TV set, watching a guest chef trying to overcome the Italian Iron Chef—I forget his name—the plump one who always wore shorts. The secret ingredient was crickets.

He looked over at me. "Oh, it's, uh, you," he said.

"Yeah, it's me again. You never did sign those books for us."

"Maybe tomorrow. I'll, uh, I'll come by your table tomorrow."

"So," I said, "you have it!"

"Yes"—and then, realizing what he'd just said—"Uh, no! Uh, have what?"

"The book, I presume."

"How, uh, how did you know?"

"Why else would you be dickering with Freddie the Cur? The only question I have is this: how did you get it?"

"What do you, uh, mean?" Brody asked.

"Well, if you killed Lissa for it, you know, I could understand. She was a nasty little woman. But…."

"I didn't kill her! I didn't."

"Then you must have seen who did," I said.

"It was, uh, it was your Margie," he said.

"I don't think so."

"But, but, she was the last one to leave the room."

"Then who was the first one?" I asked. "Obviously, you must have seen something, Brody. Otherwise, you wouldn't be drinking yourself to death."

He looked around the room until his eyes fixated on Foyle. "What do I, uh, say, Gully? *What do I say?*"

"Leave him alone!" she said, stepping forward and putting her arms around him. She cradled his head on her breasts. "He's had quite enough. Can't you see that he's so scared that he's cracking up? He's afraid of Freddie and he's afraid of the person he saw.

"Yes, there was someone else who visited Lissa last evening. He saw them leave, but he didn't recognize who it was, or even get more than a glimpse of an outline—just enough to tell that somebody was there."

"Then how did he wind up with the book?"

"She left it with him for safekeeping."

"Lissa?" I asked.

"She figured that if she kept it in her room, it could easily be stolen from her. Brody was innocuous.

Everyone knew he was flat broke. So, she offered to pay for his room and for all the booze he drank while he was here, if he kept the book safe. That was fine with him."

"So, where is it now?"

"We, uh, gave it to that Lieutenant when he interviewed us earlier today."

"And he bought your story?"

"It's the truth."

I looked straight into her cold, blue eyes. "Everyone lies," I said. "Little kids aged two, they lie. Old men in their nineties, they lie. Priests lie, and so do cops and judges and pillars of society. Men and women and children and, I suspect, even hermaphrodites. They all lie. It's just a question of when and how much and why.

"My bullshitometer just started ringing its fool head off, lady. I think *you're* lying—I'm not sure about what, and I'm not certain what your motives are, but something here just doesn't add up. I'm going to find out what it is, and when I do, we'll know the real truth, won't we?"

She didn't flinch, didn't move an inch. "Even *you* lie, you and that old lesbian bitch of yours. *You don't scare me.* Brody's done nothing wrong. I'll give you a truth straight up, if you want one: you hurt him, and I'll hurt you. Got it? Let this go. Just walk away."

"I can't do that," I said. "Margie's a friend. She doesn't deserve to be unjustly accused by the cops of something she didn't do. I'll keep on digging until I find the real dirt. And I don't care whether you or

Brody or anyone else gets nicked in the process."

"Then to hell with you! To hell with you all!" she said.

"What's, uh, the matter, Gully?" Brody asked.

"Nothing, my dear boy, nothing you need to worry yourself over. Your, uh, friend was just leaving."

"Goodbye," he said, "good luck!" He raised a bottle of beer in my direction.

That was the last time I ever saw him.

CHAPTER ELEVEN
"TEUFELSHAUS"

SATURDAY, MARCH 26

"'Take that!' Sabatini said, lunging at his opponent, the nefarious Count Alger de Mandeville.

"Mandeville parried with the rare neuvième, *and then lunged with the equally unusual* seizième *thrust, aimed at his enemy's privateers.*

"Il Signore del Castello Raffaele countered with the terrible Teufelshaus *maneuver, which not only blocked Le Comte's odd attack, but skewered him like a Viennese sausage on the end of his hard steel blade.*

"'I've always wanted to try that!' Sabatini said to his quivering Quixote, now coughing out his life on the black-and-white marble tiles of Castle Dreadlock.

"'I've…never…heard…of…such…a… thing,' the dying count gasped.

"'I read it in a book somewhere,' Il Signore said, 'Scélérate-Mouche!'

"'The...Villainous...Fly?' Mandeville died with a frown of perpetual puzzlement framing his florid face.

"'Well, perhaps the accent...?' The swordsman laughed out loud with a 'ha, ha, ha' of triumph—and then again—and again! For alas, it was very true that Sabatini was born with the gift of laughter, and a sense that the world was mad."

—*The Lord of the Castle,*
by Don Pedro Pistón (1960)

It's amazing how you can see things one way, and think you understand everything about a situation; and because you've misinterpreted or misread one small event, you get things completely wrong from the start. And then you continue down the wrong road until some strong shock jolts you wide awake again.

I thought myself another Sam Spade or Ellery Queen or even, *mon ami*, that *bon homme* detective, Hercule Poirot. I should have realized I was just another bookseller who'd read too many '50s paperbacks down the years.

I wanted to talk to Freddie the Cur, but when I pounded on his door, also located on the dark side of the motel, there was no answer.

Kitty Gaylord and Cole Spayze popped out of their room, two doors down from Freddie's, and ambled

toward me. "You looking for Freddie?" Cole said.

"You know where he is?" I asked.

"He usually hangs out this time of night in the Drinkery" (the Royal Crest's bar, next door to the Eatery).

Sure enough, I found him there plopped in the back of an oversized booth, slouched over a bloody Mary, like he was protecting it from being stolen.

"Whadya want?" he growled up at me.

"I saw your little run-in with Brody earlier this evening," I said.

"So?"

"You seemed awfully, uh, anxious about something."

"That drunken idiot," Freddie said. "First he tells me he's got something valuable that he wants to sell, and then when I meet him at the Tiger, he says he hasn't got it now. So yeah, I was angry. Wasted my time, didn't he?"

"What was that about a threat?"

He laughed, long and loud, a giant wheeze of a breeze that sounded like a dying vacuum cleaner.

"He accused me of unethical business practices," Freddie said. "Yeah, right, like he was so above-board about everything he's ever done. I mean, who *really* wrote *The O-Man?* Brody may have had a hand in it, but it doesn't read like anything else he ever produced."

"You saying he had a ghost writer?" I asked.

"I *know* he had one," the bookdealer said. "And when I mentioned that little fact to him, he got real holier-than-thou, and started telling me that he'd file

a formal complaint about the way I'd handled some of his manuscripts. Well, they *were* pure crap, and yeah, they didn't bring much, but Dameen's not exactly a well-known name any longer, is he? He wouldn't let me handle the real hot potato, the original typescript of his one bestseller—because that would reveal him to be a fraud."

"Then who *did* write *The O-Man*?"

"That's *my* secret," Freddie said. "And then he turns around and says he *has* the book after all. I don't even think he knew what he was saying by then."

"*Which* book?" I asked.

"You know which book: I don't have to tell *you* anything—you know it all. Now, let me finish my drink in peace."

* * * * * * *

When I got back to my room, I was surprised to find Margie waiting for me. "You're free!" I said, not being able to think of anything witty or even appropriate. I invited her in, and I sat on the bed while she took the only chair.

"Luvitti got me arraigned in Night Court, I pleaded 'Not Guilty,' and the judge set a bond I was able to meet. Thank the stars! I wouldn't have wanted to spend the rest of the night in that god-awful place.

"Oh, what were you able to find out—anything?"

I gave her a brief rundown on my activities after she was arrested. "The problem is," I said, "I haven't gotten anywhere, not really, except that every question I ask

seems to make the situation worse. I have no doubt that Freddie would kill for the right property, if he thought he could get away with it, I distrust Gully Foyle, and I don't know what to think about Brody Dameen. He's drunk half the time, but how much of that is fake?"

"You think they were talking about *Castle Dred*?" she asked.

"I don't know, not for sure. Probably, but every so often, I wonder."

"Do you think the cops have actually found anything to incriminate me—or anyone else?"

"Don't know that, either. Pfisch is sure as hell not going to confide in someone like me. And while he may have arrested you, I wonder how much he's actually got on you other than circumstantial evidence. I mean, did they find anything in your room?"

"Not that they told me about. They grilled me for an hour, that's all, and said they had my fingerprints in Lissa's room, on her furniture, on the door, and a few other places—but I'd already admitted being there. My attorney seems to think they've got nothing, really; I'm just convenient. He doubts that the case will actually go to trial unless they turn up something really awful."

"Like the book."

"Like the book," she said. "But nobody actually seems to *have* the book, despite what everybody is saying. If they have it, why haven't 'they' produced it?—and by *they*, I mean the cops, and Brody, and Gully, and Freddie—the lot of them. Where is it? Lissa apparently had the signed copy that first day, when she

read out loud from the inscription: it sounded a lot like what I remembered my friend writing. But where did it go?"

"You know, I remember what she said, and the first words didn't make much sense to me. 'Look sharp!'?"

"Actually, that's what convinced me it was the real thing," Margie said. "See, it was all a joke. We'd made up these outlandish pen names for ourselves. I was Lucretia Sharpe, and she was Twilla Curtayne. And then wrote these two gothics, like what Ace was starting to produce, or like *Rebecca*, Daphne du Maurier's novel, which we both loved passionately—and sent them off as individual submissions. Hers was called *Castle Dred*—the editor later added the fore-title. Mine was *Teufelshaus* or something like that."

"*Devil's Manor*," I said.

"We thought we were very clever, very witty girls playing at being writers."

"So, what happened to your book?"

"I, uh, I don't remember," she said.

I looked right at her, and I thought to myself, *Aha!—you've just out-and-out lied to me, Margie, and I would really like to know why.*

CHAPTER TWELVE
"THE AUTHORITY FILE"

SATURDAY, MARCH 26

*"If you really want to know anythin' about
me, probably the first thing would be where I
was born and all that s***, and how I f***ed
up my worthless parents' lives by being born,
and where I was edicated and what I lerned,
etc., etc.; but if you really, really want to find
that crap, you can look it up jus' like any other
rube, if you jus' want to know the truth, in the*
Who's Who *or* The Authority File. *Jus' don't
come askin' me, 'cause I don't know nothin'—
and I don't care neither."*

—*The Catcher in the Outfield,*
by Anonymous (1950)

Margie soon pleaded fatigue, and went next door
to her room, while I decided to do some digging. I
powered up my laptop computer, and did some on-line
searches I should have tried earlier.

The first name I typed in was "Twilla Curtayne"—

and there, of course, was *The Secret of Castle Dred*, which was mentioned on several websites, including one that tracked all the covers and stock numbers of the Ace paperback line. I found nothing else—and no other publications—listed under that name on the Net.

I also checked the *Catalog of Copyright Entries*, which was published by the U.S. Copyright Office. The Office itself only maintained an online database beginning in 1978, when the copyright law changed; but the old printed *Catalog*, which was in the public domain, had been scanned by Google, and was listed in alphabetical order in half-year segments.

Sure enough, I quickly found Ms. Curtayne, listed as a pseudonym of Wilhelmina Lamberth, with *Castle Dred* being copyrighted by Ace. I searched and searched and searched, but there was nothing else listed under the Curtayne name. Then I had an idea: I tried "Lamberth" instead.

In 1965 I found one entry for a W. Mina Lamberth, author of a gothic called *Devilton* published by Lancer Books under the pen name Lucrezia [sic] Sharpe. How very strange! Had Lamberth borrowed her friend's pseudonym to use on books issued by another publisher? There was nothing else in the *Catalog* under Lamberth that seemed to fit this author.

So I tried searching "Sharpe," and in 1966 found a reference from that name to Mina Maltese, author of the Lancer gothic, *Terror at Scarborough House*. I kept searching through the *Catalog* for at least another decade, until I was sure I'd located everything. She'd

used the Sharpe name for the half-dozen gothics she wrote for Lancer, and also had penned a few other books in the same genre for Paperback Library as "Bettina Bosley." Altogether, she'd published at least a dozen of these novels.

I continued my research by plugging the name Maltese into the database, but starting in 1969, the *Catalog* was filled with entries for a bunch of porn novels under that name—and I didn't think from the subject matter that this could be the same writer.

In 1975 I found a strange entry for a gothic issued by Popular Library, Ned Pines's old imprint—a writer named Lucina Sharp, pseudonym of M. M. Tolley, had penned a novel called *The Widow of Templeton Moor*. A second novel under the same pen name for the same imprint was called *Dreadstone Manor*. Could this be a coincidence?

I found a brief description of *Dreadstone* on an internet site devoted to the modern gothic, and the plot sounded roughly similar to that of *Castle Dred*. But then, many of the elements in these publications *were* very much alike, deliberately so, since that's what the fans wanted. Curiously, the story line of *Castle Dred* was actually quite different from the later norm, when considered in that light.

I'd never actually seen any of Margie's early books—at least, anything that she acknowledged as having written during her career as a paperback editor and writer. She usually dismissed her efforts during those years as not worthy of mention. I *was* aware of

one later work she penned under her real name—a cookbook devoted to berries (huckleberries, blueberries, boysenberries, dingleberries, and such)—it was a moderate success.

Just for the hell of it, I looked up that book on the Copyright Office's on-line database version of the *Catalog*, and found it registered there under "Margie Brittleback," the name I'd known her by for at least two decades. I also checked the Library of Congress on-line catalog, and *The Merry Berry Book* was recorded under her real name.

I noticed a cross-reference to an "Authority File," whatever that was, and clicked on the entry. The link took me to another catalog, which showed the author's full name as Margaret M. Brittleback, born 1945.

The berry cookbook had been published just over a decade ago as a spiral-bound trade paperback. I tried searching the other pseudonym and real names used by Margie's friend in the LC databases, but although several were listed as part of the library's paperback collection, none of these books had received full cataloging, and the names on the title pages were not cross-referenced to any other moniker.

All of this was very strange. I wondered then if Margie's tale of separation from her former girlfriend had actually been true. Maybe she was still part of her life in some way, and maybe that woman was present here at the paperback show.

But if she was, how would I find her?

CHAPTER THIRTEEN
"I WAS JUST TAKING A WALK"

SUNDAY, MARCH 27

"When Mr. Fredo Burgess of Bug Hollow announced that he would shortly be celebrating his eleventh birthday, there was much talk about his mental state in Bugganvillia.

"And when he disappeared following the piebald wizard's gaudy appearance on February the 19th, folks wondered about his stability as well.

"A hundred years later, after many and numerous quasi-adventures that we shall not detail here, since they mostly didn't amount to anything, Mr. Fredo walked into his old bungalow, now occupied by his cousin, Borgo, and announced, 'Well, I'm back.'

"'Where have you been?' Borgo's wife Buddleia asked.

"'I was just taking a walk,' Mr. Burgess said, and that was the end of it—at least for

*him—because they got an eviction order, and
sent him packing—and good riddance too!"*

—*There and Back Again,*
by Reginald Tolstoy (1955)

An hour or two later, I woke from a deep sleep to
the sound of sirens blaring and the flash-flash-flash of
red-and-white lights, and rushed to my window. The
parking lot was filled with police cars, fire engines,
and ambulances. I threw on some clothes, and headed
outside.

When I leaned over the railing of the balcony, I could
see a group of uniformed cops and attendants gathered
around a prone figure near the foot of the metal-and-
concrete bottom steps.

"What is it?" Margie said behind me.

I turned and looked at her. She was breathing hard,
as if she'd been running. I noticed that she was still
fully dressed.

"Where were you?" I asked.

"I was, uh, just taking a walk."

"Uh-huh."

"I was talking to a friend, all right?" she said, "on
the other side of the motel."

Down below, one of the medical personnel covered
the body with a sheet, and then walked away from
the corpse. The police formed a perimeter around the
scene, pushing all the spectators back. I didn't have my
watch on, but I think it was around one in the morning.

Margie unlocked the door on her room, and vanished

inside. She was back again five minutes later.

"Kimmy at the desk says it's Brody Dameen!" she said.

"I thought it was Karen at the desk," I said.

"No, that was last night. Kimmy has the night shift on Saturday."

Kimmy, Karen, Denise—it was all the same to me. I mentioned something about the graveyard shift turning into a real horror story, and she just looked at me crooked, like I'd crawled out from under a rock somewhere. Women! They had no sense of humor at all.

"I wonder if he fell—or was pushed," I said.

"You always think the worst of people."

"Still...."

Then I saw Lieutenant Pfisch emerge from a newly-arrived black sedan, and I knew we were in for a long night. After watching him for a few minutes, I returned to my room, and crawled back into bed.

* * * * * * *

I was up early the next morning, waking with the sun. After a quick shower, I dressed and went outside again. Dameen's body was finally gone—I could see the markings where it had fallen. There were a couple of investigators closely examining the first-floor balcony and the stairwell leading up to it. I was so intent on the man and woman conducting the search that I didn't hear the Lieutenant coming up behind me.

"Good morning," he said. "Couldn't sleep, eh?"

I straightened up abruptly. "Not after last night," I said.

"Where were you when Brody fell?"

"Asleep in my bed."

"Anyone who can corroborate that?" the cop asked.

"The bedbugs? Look, Pfisch, I usually sleep alone. I laid down sometime after eleven—didn't catch the clock, sorry—and the next I knew was when you folks showed up."

"What about your girlfriend?"

"You mean Margie? She's *not* my girlfriend. She's a business partner and friend, but that's all." I was getting a bit irritated at all the questions.

"Oh, because she's gay?" he said. When he saw the look on my face, he added: "Yeah, I know. In fact, I think it's pretty common knowledge around here. Where *was* she?"

"I have no idea. You'd have to ask her that."

"Well, I did," Pfisch said, "and she was pretty vague in her response. What did *you* see?"

"She was out there with me watching the scene early this morning. I don't know where she was before or after that."

"What do you know about Gully Foyle, Dameen's significant other?" he asked.

I was about to say something, and then realized that I didn't really know much at all. She'd shown up with Brody just for this con, and had been introduced to me as his "friend," but she'd said nothing at all about her background. I told Pfisch that, and he just grunted.

"Didn't say much to me either," he finally said, "but we're looking into her past."

"You think...?"

"I don't think anything," he said. "We're just doing what we always do: question people, check their stories and alibis, and see what else we can find out about them. The same is true of you."

"*Me*? What do you mean?"

"You've read enough of those paperback novels of yours to know the drill: everyone's a suspect, at least at first. If Brody was killed—and we're not sure yet— then almost anyone here could have done it."

"You think maybe he just tripped?" I asked.

"Well, he, uh, did over-imbibe." That was a word I hadn't heard in ordinary conversation in a very long time.

"Yes," I said, "but he almost never went anywhere without Gully, even when he was drinking."

"Well, she claims she was asleep, and didn't know he was absent from their room."

"Then what was he doing out there in the middle of the night?"

"Well, that's the pertinent question, isn't it?" Pfisch said. "By the way, I finished reading that book you sold me. I wondered about something."

"Yes?"

"In the first part of the book, Jezebel comes upon her father slumped in his great-chair. She asks him what's wrong, and he admits that the imminent defeat of the South in the Civil War will destroy them financially,

since the bonds he purchased are now nearly worth-less. She climbs onto his lap—this supposed twenty-two-year-old woman—puts her arms around his neck, kisses him, and says that everything will be all right, that she's been approached several times by Colonel Montragora to work for him as a governess. She says she'll do anything to save him—anything!

"Even without a detailed description of what was actually happening, the scene made me very uncomfortable, because it felt to me very much like some of the cases of child abuse that I used to investigate when I served with the Family Services Unit. *I* think that the author based this particular passage on something that happened to her in real life—it has that immediacy—and I just wondered if you knew anything about it."

To tell the truth, I didn't remember that particular section, so many years after the fact, and I told him so—but I said I'd examine the passage again.

"I'd appreciate it," Pfisch said. "Oh, yeah, and I'd prefer you keeping this to yourself."

CHAPTER FOURTEEN
"SOMETIME AFTER MIDNIGHT"

SUNDAY, MARCH 27

"Consulting detective Émile Friand gazed around at the faces looking up at him. One of these individuals was a cold-blooded killer who'd systematically murdered sixteen members of the University community. He marveled again at the perversity of the human soul. These persons had done bad, bad things to their fellow humans.

"But who was it? There was the mild-mannered library cataloger, Ms. Figgit, who always appeared uncomfortable in social settings. Next to her sat Dr. Stürn, Professor of Judicial Science, known for his raspy nature and uncompromising standards. On the other side of the librarian was Dr. Holiday, Dean of Humanities; and beyond her Dr. Perryguard, Professor of Anthropography; and then Dr. Krikor, Head of Armenian Studies; and Dr. Offell, Provost of the University. And completing

the circle on the other side, he saw Dr. Fribæse, Chair of the Faculty Senate; Dr. Tsingtsong, Chair of Arabian Studies; Mr. Dámaso, Head of Cafeteria Services; and Lieutenant Ynorr, Chief of the Campus Police. Standing behind them all were several of Ynorr's armed officers.

" 'You must understand,' Friand began, 'that this was a very difficult case; and I do regret the loss of fifteen more lives while I was trying to unravel the first death—of the custodian of the Fifth Floor. As you may recall, Mr. Pëtr was found chopped into pieces and stuffed into his own refuse cart. I initially thought that his death was either an accident or suicide, but was forced to change my mind after the additional bodies began turning up around campus.

" 'What did these multitudinous victims have in common? Ah, that was the difficulty: to find the missing link, so to speak. I uncovered the key clue on the day when I was forced to eat on campus during an unexpected rainstorm, and found the food utterly disgusting and inedible. When I protested that fact to Mr. Dámaso, he said that I should 'Go fish!'

" 'Those were the words written on the wall in ketchup above victim #6, Dr. Quarton—which I originally believed indicated the religious preferences of the killer. Perhaps I should have interpreted the sign more literally.

"'Therefore, I can now identify the murderer without any doubt. It was...'—my audience leaned forward expectantly—'...it was... Lieutenant Ynorr!'

"'What?' the policeman said. 'You must be crazy.'

"'Ah, no, you are the demented one, officer. Only you *were available sometime after midnight on each of the days when a victim was killed. Lack of sleep can lead to serious psychological breakdowns—this is a well-known fact. It had to be you!'*

"'No, no, no!' Dámaso shouted, jumping to his feet. 'You don't understand! I was a culinary genius—and none of you, not one, recognized my talent. You pooh-poohed my deviled tripe, you turned your collective noses down at my curried chicken tartare, you thought my fried and powdered road kill helper was poopeepie. Well, I showed you, didn't I? The dish I served today, my Bon Homme Richard Appétit, represents new heights of culinary delight. Ha, ha, ha—and you thought it was pork! Ha, ha, ha.'

"'Anyway, it was a good theory,' Friand said. 'I will send you my bill in the morning.'

"And with that, the petit little French Guyanan made a formal bow, and exited stage left."

—The Case of the Curious Cuisine,
by Stanley Earl Silverstein (1958)

Margie and I usually met over an early breakfast at the Eatery, before going into the exhibit hall, but she didn't make an appearance that morning; and I was sitting there sipping my cup of hot tea and picking at my toast when Freddie the Cur plopped down across from me, along with the old paperback hacks, Ferdinand Bartholomew and Kitty Gaylord. Ferd had written a hundred novels for Dell, Belmont, Beeline, and several other houses, and Kitty had done "nursies" and other romances for Ace, Harlequin, and Popular Library.

"What a shame," Freddie said, after being served a stack of hotcakes, three eggs, bacon and sausage, and biscuits and gravy. The other two ordered more reasonable portions.

"You mean about Brody?" I asked.

"Yeah. Poor guy really had a problem."

"You two ever resolve your, uh, business arrangement?" I said.

"Oh, sure," he said, "I took care of that last night."

"I thought he didn't have what you wanted."

"Well, he found it again," Freddie said. "We met next door at the Drinkery, late."

"*How* late?"

He looked at me with his small reptilian eyes, and squinted: "I've already been through this with Pfisch, and I don't really want to ruin my first meal of the day. It's what gets me going, you know? So let it lay! We did a deal, I've got the book, he got the money, and that's that, honey. You can ask Daryl M. next door, and he'll

tell you that Brody paid off his tab last night."

"Indeed?"

"Yes, he did seem quite happy when he left the bar," Kitty said. She was a woman in her sixties, with gray hair and jowls.

"I saw him too," Bartholomew said. He and Kitty often palled around together. "He did pay his bill, just like Freddie said. That was before he left."

"Did he show the book to you?" I asked.

"Nah," Ferdinand said, "he just told me that he'd forgotten where he'd put it, but Gully had found it for him, and it was quite rare, 'worth a lot of dough,' as he so quaintly put it. He was rushing off to meet the buyer."

"Just a minute," I said. "He indicated to you that he was leaving the Drinkery to make the sale?"

"Yeah," both Ferd and Kitty said.

"Well, that just isn't the way it happened," Freddie the Cur said. "We did our deal earlier in the evening, and I paid him several thousand cash money too. It was a good clean copy."

"A good clean copy of *what*?" I asked.

"I'll have it on display at my table when we open," he said. "You're welcome to come by and make a bid."

"Maybe I will." I turned back to the two writers: "So, who was this other buyer, and what was Brody selling?"

"He didn't say," Kitty indicated.

Bartholomew just shrugged his shoulders. He was engrossed in dipping his toast into the runny parts

of his eggs, and slurping up the remains. Finally, he looked up and said: "I didn't know about the other book, whatever it was. Brody was always surprisingly cagey about such things. But he had a knack for finding stuff, that's for sure. Hey, Kitty, remember that boondoggled photo-illustrated edition of *Forever Amber*? Man, now *that* was really something!"

"What time did Brody leave?" I asked.

"Oh, God, I don't know," Bartholomew said. "I mean, we were drinking ourselves, you know?"

"Sometime after midnight," Kitty said. "I remember, because we made a joke about the day, and that it was now Sunday."

"So, not long before Dameen took his tumble," I said.

"I suppose not. I don't know when he died," she said.

"Well, it was about one when the commotion woke me up," I said. "So, it had to be before that."

"I guess it was, then," Ferd said. "Well, it's just too damned...you know. Brody went through spells when he was sober, and he told me a few weeks ago that his new girlfriend, Gilly or whatever her name is, she'd really helped clean up his act."

"Then why was he back on the sauce?" I asked.

"Who the hell gives a fuck?" Freddie the Cur said. He was shoveling the end of an apple sausage down his gullet, and the act was so disgusting that I had to look away. I wondered if I'd ever be able to eat one again myself. He belched out loud. "He was just a poor drunk, OK, who couldn't help himself. Yeah, he could

be fun at times, and I've seen him mean as a skunk, too. He used to beat his wife back in the old days. I bet that Gully didn't let him do that."

"Why do you say that?" I asked.

"I heard her telling him off yesterday," he said, burping again, and shifting his ass to exhale a fragrant cloud. "He was begging her to forgive him—again. She really had the man pussy-whipped, if you know what I mean. He would have done anything for that dame."

"What did she say, specifically?" I pressed.

"Oh, just that if someone was still alive—I didn't catch the name—she'd take care of him all right, just like she'd done to someone else. She was just reaming him out, man, right and left—and I could see that he was terrified that she'd leave him. I had the impression that they hadn't been together more than a month or two. Finally, they made up, she kissed him lightly on the cheek, and told him to go do what she'd said— and I don't know what that was. That was right after we'd finished our business in the Drinkery. She'd been hiding in a booth to one side."

"She was waiting for you to finish the transaction."

"That's what I said. What a wimpy little twerp he was—no balls at all. Didn't used to be that way. That's what drink'll do to you." Then he glanced down at his watch. "Jeezus, it's later than I thought. Gotta go meet somebody before I open up.

"You'll take care of this, right?" he said, nodding at me. "Thanks!" He was up and gone before I could

reply, surprisingly fast for an oversized tank. I never saw him alive again.

CHAPTER FIFTEEN
"YOU'RE NOT MY HUSBAND"

SUNDAY, MARCH 27

" '*You're not my husband,'* Cissy Malaparte, the Head of Procurement, said. '*However, you'll do in a, uh, pinch'*—*and with that she leaned over, grabbed Craig's double chin, and squeezed*—*hard!*

" '*Ouch!' he said. 'Miss Malaparte, this isn't really kosher. I mean....'*

" '*Oh, common, Craigie, I'm just looking for a little fun here.'*

" '*But I already have a friend,' he said. 'This just isn't right.'*

" '*No, but it sure would feel good, wouldn't it?' She stroked the pointed auburn sideburn snaking down the left side of his cheek. 'Oh, my!'*

"*She got up from behind her desk, walked over to the door, and locked it from inside. Then she unfastened the top button on her blouse, and moistened her lips.*

"'Don't you find me just a little sexy?' the sixty-year-old executive asked.

"'Uh, well, uh, of course, but....'

"'But what, Craigie?'

"'But, Miss Malaparte, you're not my husband!'

"'Huh?' Then she looked at him more carefully, noticed the way he dressed and handled himself, and finally said, 'Oh.'

"'The heart is a lonely hunter,' she muttered, motioning him to leave.

"That was just the way the fortune cookie crumbled sometimes, on the other side of...The Plastic Ceiling!"

—*The Plastic Ceiling*,
by Demeter S. Runnin (1965)

When I got back to the exhibit area, and showed security my pass, I saw that Margie was already setting up for the morning.

"Where *were* you?" I asked.

"I had stuff to do," she said.

When I looked at her sideways, she straightened up and said: "*What!* Look, I'm under a lot of stress. You're not my husband; you're not even my boyfriend, as if I'd want such a thing. We're in business together, that's it. I don't have to account to you for my time."

"No," I said, "you don't, but I did think you were a friend."

"You...I...*you are*! You're still my friend. It's just

that this has been a really lousy con, and I'm, well, I'm *afraid*! I didn't do what the police think I did, but I have no way of proving it. And you haven't gotten any further yourself, have you?"

"Well, I might have," I said. "Margie, you haven't told me the complete story about you and your friend four decades ago, and I really think I need to know."

"I *can't* tell you," she said. "I made a promise, many years ago, and I believe in keeping those kinds of commitments."

"Even if your friend is dead."

"Even then," she said. "But I don't know that. Really."

"You told me that you didn't recognize your friend here at the show, as she might be now," I said.

"I've looked and I've looked," Margie said, "but the only person that seems to me to bear any resemblance to her at all couldn't possibly *be* her—just couldn't."

"And who's *that*?" I asked.

"Well, it's nothing, really, but Gully Foyle said something the other day that sorta reminded me of my old town. She doesn't look or act anything like my, uh, friend did, so I don't think she's related to her in any way; but something in her speech echoed in my mind, and just for a moment, I was taken back to where I was born…."

"Interesting," I said. "Nobody seems to know much about Ms. Foyle."

"…I'm not even sure what it was, exactly," Margie said, talking over me, "but something that I can't put my finger on. It'll come to me. I hate getting old!"

"Me, too," I said. "We might as well be married, half the time."

She looked at me funny, and then said: "I don't think so. You'd drive me crazy."

Then the doors of the room opened, and the hoards of collectors came swarming over the tables, like a rush of army ants looking for any tidbits that they could scavenge. We'd put out a few "loss leaders" at the front of our table, including Lovisi's stapled *Gurgles* paperback (we'd already sold the sequels), a detailed bibliography of Maltese's triple century of published pb works by the indefatigable Boden "B.C." Clarke, Kurland and Lupoff's double, Lupoff and Kurland's second double, Kupoff Lurland's double-double, a tell-all bio of Poul Anderson by his comely wife, Pronzini's untitled and nonbylined mystery (very rarely seen), Nolan's horrible horror of horrors, Turtledove's one hundredth installment of his Endless War series ("The war, the war!"), Evans's *Doggie Bites*, Glut's *Frankly Spoken*, Beagle's *Unicorn Cookery in 135 Easy Lessons (with Illustrations), and an Audio Tape by the Author, Who Will Explain Himself Oh So Carefully and at Great Length, with Additional Explications by His Assistant)*, Brandner's *Harry Tails and the Howling Good Time*, Arthur Byron's cover (signed a dozen times), and several others.

They were all scooped up within minutes—thankfully.

The morning sales alone easily made up for the generally slow days we'd had on Friday and Saturday.

I guess it's true what they say: paperback collectors do worship the good books.

About eleven o'clock Gully and Kitty came wandering by, talking with their heads close together. I didn't even know that they were friends.

"Good morning, ladies," I said. "Can I interest you in some paperbacks?"

Gully glanced over at me. "That depends on the book," she said. She didn't particularly look like the grieving girlfriend to me.

"I was sorry to hear…."

She held up her hand. "I appreciate your sentiments," she said, "but I'm trying to get on with my life. I'd only known Brody for a short time, after all."

"How long?" I asked.

"What?" She frowned.

"I said: how long did you know Brody?"

"I met him at the WWA assembly earlier this year."

"Oh, and what were you doing there?" I asked.

"Well, uh, you know, I'm interested in paperback westerns," Gully said.

"Really?" Margie said. "You never said anything to me."

"Me either," Kitty piped up.

"That's usually a genre favored by male readers," I said.

"Women can be interested in such things too," Gully said.

"It's just unusual, that's all," I said.

"Yeah, well, there it is. Go sit on it! Come on,

Kitty—I'm not going to get any sympathy here, that's for sure."

When they walked away, I turned to Margie: "Was it something I said?"

"I found that whole exchange very queer," she said, "very strange indeed."

CHAPTER SIXTEEN
"GIRL FRIDAY"

SUNDAY, MARCH 27

"She came from the Bayou country, a place of gators and skeeters and funny-talking Frenchies. But she was determined to make it in the big city—Texarkana, Arkansas (or was it Texas?), and to send whatever money she made back to her poor old Mama in Voyoute, Louisiana.

"'Hulotte!' her boss, Mr. Ginrak, said, 'bring me a pencil, please.'

"He noticed me, she thought to herself. He wants a pencil! And she carefully picked up the best implement she could find, and sharpened it right down to a perfect point.

"'Here you are, sir,' she said, a half hour later.

"'Uh, thanks, but I already got one for my-self.'

"'But...but...,' and then she started to cry.

"'What is it, Hulotte?'

"'I try so hard, sir, to become a Girl Friday, but I never seem to make it past Thursday! Not ever!'

"'Don't be sad,' he said. 'Even though I'm laying you off tomorrow, you can still be my special friend. I won't let you get lost on the streets. Why, you can come live with me!'

"'Really and truly! I can become your own Girl Friday?'

"'Oh, yes, it'll be like Friday every day!'

"Poor country lass: she just didn't understand that TGIF almost never outlasted the inevitably weak end."

—*Girl Thursday,*
by DiDi Wickheiser (1963)

Just before lunch, Lieutenant Pfisch made another appearance at our display. "Can I talk with you?" he said, pulling me to one side.

"I'll be back in a minute," I told Margie, walking away with him to where we could talk without being overheard.

"Did you look at the book again?" he asked.

"I did glance at the passage you indicated," I said, "and I agree, when you read between the lines, it's suggestive of some unnatural relationship. But if this was based on some *real* father-daughter incest, the parent in this instance would have to be at least eighty-five, if not older."

"And probably dead."

"Perhaps," I said. "I'm not sure this is about that, though."

"Then what *is* it about? I still haven't cleared your partner, you know."

"I think she knows more than she's letting on, but I can't pry whatever it is loose from her. I've tried, Lieutenant."

"We've got two people dead, and we still haven't figured out who did the deed or why—and I'm not sure we've come to the end of it yet," he said. "Another thing. I can trace your friend back to the mid-1970s in the records, but not before. I know you said she worked for certain firms in the 1960s, but there's nothing that I can find that actually lists her as an editor."

"I doubt if she had that kind of status back then," I said. "She was probably an intern or editorial assistant or what they used to call a 'Girl Friday'; those folks never get shown on the company registers of publishing firms."

"Is there anybody I could ask who might have worked for one of those lines?" Pfisch said.

"Probably, but off the top of my head, I can't think of anyone. Heckelmann's dead, and so's Ned Pines. It'd have to be one of the lower-level editorial personnel, someone who was young enough to have worked there at the same time she did. Or maybe one of the authors that lived close enough to pay frequent visits to either firm. These weren't very large companies, when you come right down to it. Not back in those days."

Then I saw someone shuffle by, and yelled out,

"Marty! Marty Hughes!" When he turned around, I motioned him towards us, whispering to Pfisch, "He created some of the artwork on the books these firms published."

"Hey, good to see ya again," he said, peering at my face. His sight had faded a bit with age. "You're, uh, it'll come to me, uh...." I reminded him of my name. "Yeah, yeah, now I remember. You're Margie's friend, aren't you?"

"I am," I said. "Mr. Pfisch here is a fan of classic paperbacks, and he was wondering about the personnel at Monarch Books and Popular Library back in the 1960s. You did work for them, didn't you?"

"Oh, yeah, they didn't pay much, particularly Monarch, but I always liked working for Mr. Heckelmann. He knew what he wanted, a real pro, if you know what I mean."

"Did Margie Brittleback work for them?" I asked.

"Yeah, she was there for a couple of years, working as an aide to Mr. Heckelmann, until they started going downhill in '64. They finally closed their doors a year later. 'Course, that wasn't her actual name."

"Really?" I said.

"She called herself 'Margie,' even then, but her real name was Mina something or other, I don't remember now."

"Mina Lamberth?"

"Yeah, that was it! Lamberth! She wrote a couple of sexy books for Mr. Heckelmann under house names, and edited a few others, I seem to recall. I always

wondered how she got that kind of experience. I mean, she was just a frail little thing, very shy and naïve, not long out of high school, I don't think. She had a Southern accent back then, too, but I never met any of her relatives. I was just there once in a while, along with some others, to peddle my cover art. Mr. Heckelmann gave me some good tips."

"What about Popular Library?"

"Well, she went there after Monarch and Gold Star folded, but I don't think I ran into her there very much. I did ask her out once, but she politely refused. I think she had something else going on the side. By then, she was only known as Margie, and she was writing gothics and maybe a few other novels for houses like Lancer. I think I heard that she also worked for Midwood for several years, but I didn't do any work for them."

I thanked Marty for his time, and asked him to come by our table to autograph a few of the books that featured his cover art.

"So, who's this Mina?" Pfisch asked.

I told him about my searches through the various bibliographical databases, and what I'd found there.

"You think maybe there was no friend, just her?"

"I don't know," I said. "I still think we're missing something vital here. I just wish the hell I knew what it was."

I left the Lieutenant standing there, gazing after me with a frown on his face. Suddenly, I almost chuckled. I had the thought, I don't know from where, that he looked like he'd been sideswiped by a wet, slimy fish,

right across the ole kazoo. Pfisch-fish, get it?

Then I stopped by our display briefly, and told Margie I was going out to pick up some lunch for us.

CHAPTER SEVENTEEN
"YOU CAN'T DO THAT"

SUNDAY, MARCH 27

"The Bardol Brothers loved robbing trains: big ones, little ones, it made no difference. Truth be told, they just liked playing with the things. If they'd grown up near a town that had had railroad service, they probably all would have wound up as engineers, brakemen, conductors, and such. But Perdunk, Wyoming, shared the dubious record of being located the furthest distance from a rail line of any town in the U.S. of A.

"So, they had to go looking for them, and since they never had been trained for any gainful work, they robbed them, combining both of their interests into a single pastime.

"It was Bustap Bardol, the second of the boys, who had the brilliant idea: 'Saay,' he said, 'why don't we go steal ourselves a train!?'

"'Yeah,' Brother Bart said, 'why not? Then we wouldn't have to keep movin' around from

place to place. We could just keep drawing our cash from the same place all the time.'

" 'Yeah!' they all agreed. So they went looking for the ideal heist.

"It was Beau Bardol who figured it out. 'See, if we hijack a train from a short line, the agents will track us down, 'cause, well, they don't have but a short ways to go. But if we do one from the Transcon, they'd have to look across the whole blasted country to find us.'

"Beau's irrefutable logic carried the day, and a few weeks later, the Brothers boarded a Frisco Western train heading west from Kansas City, and quickly took control.

" 'We want you to take us to Perdunk, Wyoming,' Brother Bret said.

" 'I can't do that. There's no line that goes there,' the engineer replied.

"About that time, the federals stopped the train at Grand Terrace, near the Food Connection, and arrested the entire gang.

" 'What happened?' Brother Brent asked his siblings inside the Palouse County clink.

" 'We forgot one thing: you can't get there from here unless your there is already here.'

" 'Huh?' they all said. Even in Perdunk, Wyoming, Bardol was not a synonym for smart."

—The Great Brain Robbery,
by John M. Crichton (1969)

And that brings us around full circle, back to where we started, with Freddie the Cur being impaled through his teeny-weeny little knot of a black heart right behind his own table, in public view of everyone. Who would do such a thing, and why? I had a pretty good idea by this point, but I couldn't prove a thing.

Of course, Lieutenant Pfisch immediately shut down the Paperback Show, permanently this time, and ordered all of us to gather in the Bloomberg Auditorium, a large room adjoining the Nelson Display Center, under the close supervision of his officers, who were now being constantly augmented with reinforcements.

Margie and I brought lunch with us, and continued to munch and sip while the rest of our immediate audience gazed at us with unbridled lust and gluttony. We just smiled at them, we two: the happy—the full—business couple belching straightforwardly into the future on Johnny-burgers and roast beef melts.

"When do you think they'll allow us to retrieve our stock?" Bartleby asked. "I've got some valuable stuff setting out in public view."

"Probably never," I said, "at least until they solve the murders."

That shut him up. He scribbled something down on a piece of paper, the little twerp.

"We want DNA samples from all of you," Pfisch announced in a loud voice. "We've found DNA residue on the scarf that strangled Melissa Boaz, and we believe it may come from her killer."

The whole room started buzzing in consternation.

"You can't do that," Ferd Bartholomew said. "You have to have our consent or something."

"We'll start with the ones who are willing," the policeman said, "and then work down to the rest of you. If we have to get warrants, we'll do so."

Suddenly Gully Foyle stood up and said in a quiet voice that carried over the entire crowd: "You don't have to do that, Lieutenant. I know that Brody killed Lissa Boaz. Even though I cared for him, I won't have anyone else accused of a crime that he committed."

"Why would he do that?" Pfisch said.

"He was seriously in the hole," she said, "and being harassed by phone calls and personal visits from debt collectors. Lissa gave him a couple of really valuable paperbacks to hold for her, in exchange for which she paid him a few hundred bucks. When she asked for them back again, so she could auction them to the highest bidder, he found himself in a bind, because he'd already arranged to mortgage the books to Freddie the Cur on the side, for enough to get caught up again. He'd have a clean slate, and then he could buy the books back from Freddie later on.

"At least, that was his idea, poor foolish man. In his later years, he never had two nickels to rub together, and I knew that, and still fell for him anyway. I would have supported him.

"So, he went to Lissa's room, and she threatened to sue him, which would have ruined his reputation, such as it was, and he killed her. He came to me afterward, and said that he didn't mean to, but it just

happened. And then he started drinking and drinking and drinking to drown the guilt, but it didn't work. He did sell the books, but I don't think he got as much from Freddie as he thought he would; and he felt like a Judas later.

"Brody was the killer," she said.

"Then who killed Brody?" the Lieutenant asked.

"*Brody* did," Gully said. "I saw it. He was drunk and he misstepped and he fell down the stairs and broke his neck—just like it appeared in the first place."

"Where were you?"

"I was a flight above him, on the landing. We'd had a terrible row, because I told him he had to turn himself in. He didn't want to. He ran away, down the stairs, and the rest just happened. I knew he was dead the moment he landed on the asphalt of the parking lot. And goddamn me, I turned my back on him and walked away. I've been walking away from people my whole life, ever since I abandoned my mother."

"What about Freddie the Cur?" Pfisch asked.

"I don't know anything about that," Gully said. "I do know Freddie had the books—there were at least two of them, that Tarzan thing and that awful gothic—and I know that Brody had a wad of money stuffed in his pants when he returned from his meeting with him, but I don't know any of the details."

"And conveniently, there's no one left to ask," the policeman said.

"As you say, Lieutenant," she said.

"Well, Ms. Foyle, I think you and I are going to

have an extended conversation about this matter, in private, along with Ms. Brittleback over there, and her 'companion' in bookselling"—he motioned to me. "The rest of you will remain here under the watchful eyes of my men. We'll escort you as needed for various personal breaks, and we'll bring you some food and water."

Fifty voices tried to talk at once, before Pfisch shouted them into silence: "Enough!" he said. "I'll get back to you once we sort this out. You *will* remain here for the time being, until I'm convinced we have a true picture of the situation. Please pass your phones and communication devices to Sergeant Hamm."

And then the four of us went off to Romper-Room—or so it seemed to me.

CHAPTER EIGHTEEN
"I DON'T BELIEVE EVERYTHING YOU'VE SAID"

SUNDAY, MARCH 27

" 'We want you to kill a geek,' he said.

"Wednesday adjusted her shoulder straps, applied more lipstick, checked the image in her mirror and the messages on her bleep, and said: 'Which Greek? I mean, jeez, I know a fat Greek named Nick. In fact, they're all named Nick!'

" 'No, no, a geek!' the much older man said. He wore a powdery gray wig that showed his dominating and commanding personality.

" 'That'll cost you more,' she purred, pulling her skirt up even further, 'much more. Geeks are smart—at least until they meet a real woman. Then their brains turn to refried beans.'

" 'That's because most of them have never met a real woman. We'll pay your price, Wednesday,' the near immortal, handsome, super-intelligent everyman said, 'but you'll have to pay ours, too.'

"She looked at him more closely. 'Really!' she said. 'I don't think you could keep up with me, Job. I mean, I can't wait for on-the-Job training, so to speak.'

"'I've had more women than you,' he said, 'and more geeks too. Nobody knows the trouble I've seen.'

"'And nobody much cares, either. I don't believe everything you've said, but still, I'll take the assignment. There's just one thing, though.'

"'What's that, Wednesday?'

"'Well, actually,' she said, puffing up her lips, 'it's not *Wednesday, it's Thursday, and you're my assignment today.' She spit the poison dart right between his eyes. He fell over head-first into his soufflé.*

"'Job one always comes first,' she said to herself, smiling. 'Mission accomplished!' she bleeped into the button fastening the top of her blouse. She left the tab on the target's bald spot, now made visible by his side-sliding wig."

—Wednesday,
by RonBob A. Haldane (1968)

"Let me begin," Pfisch said, "by saying that I don't believe everything you've said, Ms. Foyle. There may be elements of truth rattling around in there, but having observed Mr. Dameen first-hand, I don't think he could plan his way out of a paper bag. And while he

might kill someone in a burst of anger, he'd be more likely to vomit all over them.

"It's certainly possibly that his own death was just an accident; in fact, we've found nothing that would indicate to the contrary. I just find it suspicious that someone so intimately involved in all these proceedings would himself buy the farm right in the middle of things.

"And someone clearly murdered Mr. van Noland. Curiously, even though the event seemed to take place right out in the open, so to speak, no one saw anything.

"Now, you say that Ms. Boaz was killed because she wanted her books back."

"Yes, that's what Brody told me: she specifically wanted that particular novel, *Castle Dred*, that evening, because she had someone on the hook," Gully said. "She was meeting someone later that night, and he had the impression that she expected to get a good price."

"But she didn't, did she?" Pfisch said.

"No, Brody had already arranged to sell it to Freddie."

"So, what did he tell Ms. Boaz?"

"Well, I don't know exactly. He told me afterward that when he said he didn't have it close by, she blew up at him, and threatened to call in the law."

"You said originally that she was going to sue him."

"Well, maybe that too. He just indicated that she was really mad, and started making threats at him."

"So, then he killed her," the Lieutenant said.

"That's what he said."

"How, specifically?"

"Well, didn't he strangle her? That's what I've been hearing," she said.

"Hearing from who?" he asked.

"Well, you know, from everyone."

"Not from Brody?"

"Well, from him too, of course."

"What specifically did he say?" the policeman wanted to know.

"Something like, 'She's dead! I didn't mean anything. She's just…she's dead!' Then he grabbed a bottle and started chugging it."

"He didn't provide you with any details?"

"Not that I remember."

"So, why do you think that Mr. Dameen's the murderer?"

"Who else could it be? He had the book!"

"Did you ever examine that novel yourself?" Pfisch asked.

"I just glanced at it. It had some silly inscription on the title page. Didn't pay much attention, really. Never saw what the fuss was all about."

"You said the inscription was on the title page?"

"Yes."

"But Ms. Brittleback here—and several others, I might add—heard Ms. Boaz recite the inscription out loud, and they stated that it was clearly on the half-title page, or page one of the paperback."

"They did?"

"Yes, they did."

"Well, maybe it was, then."

"You don't seem to know very much about these events, for all that you've named your late boyfriend the killer."

"Well, I know what I know, Lieutenant, and I'm convinced, sorry to say, that Brody Dameen killed Lissa Boaz."

"What about Mr. van Noland?"

"What about him?"

"According to your testimony, he got the book or books from Mr. Dameen."

"Yes."

"When we went through the stock laid out on his table, and also examined the contents of his room, we found the Tarzan novel clutched in his hand—and no trace of *The Secret of Castle Dred*."

"Like I said, I don't know anything about his death."

"Do you have the book?" the policeman asked.

"No, of course not. What would I want with something like that?"

"I don't know. I don't know what anyone would want with it, unless that person was the killer."

I interrupted at this point: "Lieutenant," I said, "Mr. van Noland was not well liked in the business. He made many enemies, both among the collectors and among his fellow dealers. Maybe he tried to drive too hard a bargain for what was certainly a rarity: the only known signed copy of the first original gothic novel published in the paperback field. Anybody could have killed him."

"Yes, but that 'anybody' had to have a good enough

reason."

"To own one of a kind?—that's reason enough for certain fans. You don't know how rabid some of these folks can be."

And we went on and on from there, with Pfisch questioning Margie at length, and then Gully again—and even me—but in the end he finally decided to leave things as they were.

"Very well," he said. "We'll take you at your word, Ms. Foyle, and identify Mr. Dameen as Ms. Boaz's killer. Mr. Dameen's demise will be listed as an accidental death. And we'll continue looking for Mr. van Noland's murderer."

Of course, they never found him, and the case remains open to this day. The fiftieth Paperback Exposition and Show ground down to an ignominious end; our coordinator, Tomás Law, vowed never to return to Santo Verdugo again.

Margie and I packed away our remaining offerings, after making a couple of under-the-counter deals with our fellow bookmongers, and loaded everything back in the van. Then we went out to dinner.

EPILOGUE
"A CHORUS OF OLÉS"

SUNDAY, MARCH 27

"I spat into the face of Vimius Nuyance, Percolator of Gore. 'I'll drink iced tea before surrendering my manhood to your tutelage,' I said.

"Then I hopped onto the saddle of my chickie-poo, dug my spurs into its succulent thighs, and gripped the stirrup as the giant bird leapt into the sky.

"'Get him!' shouted the ruler, and the great pigeonators of Gore mounted their sky-steeds, beating into the airwaves after me, and chirping their chorus of 'olés'!

"'What'th it going to be then, eh, Mathter?' my luscious leaper lisped, beating her wings against the oncoming wind.

"'Fly away! Fly away,' I yelled over the swishing of the air apparent. Discretion is always the better part of valor.

"But there were just too many of them, and my chances of reaching Ailandia seemed slender to slim.

"'Release the secret weapon!' I ordered my chickie-poo, and a noxious mix of bug juice and splatter-yuck spewed out of the bird's nether end towards the oncoming flock of sky-rats.

"One by one they went 'Ewww,' and dropped out of the race, until only Vimius himself remained. I banked into a nose-dive, and went right at the climbing clodhopper, drawing my snicker-snack from its purse. The Percolator tried to react—but too late! Blood spurted all over chickie-poo and my brand new uniform, which had been carefully knitted for me by my house-frau, Wanessa. I'd have much to explain whenever I returned to home-base.

"But return I eventually did, after just three more years of wandering through the back plains of Gore—having a great time, carousing whenever I felt like it, getting plastered on fermented chickie-juice, and hanging out generally with the laddies.

"The truth is, I didn't really like the company of girls all that much. Too many tea-parties and such, too much of 'Do this' and 'Do that.' Give me the free life anytime!

"'Yeth, Mathter,' my chickie-poo agreed."

—*Buckets of Gore*, by John Lang IV

I picked a dive called Uncle Timo's, a Mexican eatery located about a mile from the motel, and I ordered their *molcajete*, a stone pot filled with strips of nopales (cactus leaves), beef, bacon, chicken, shrimp, chorizo, onions, and much else; while Margie just worried a taco salad.

I found a private booth off in one corner, underneath the TV, set to a loud Spanish-language channel, which I thought would drown out any of our conversation.

"So, what did you think of Lieutenant Pfisch's conclusions?" I asked, trying to munch down a boiling-hot strip of nopal.

"I think it's probably the best solution we're going to get," she finally said. She had her eyes firmly planted in the center of her guacamole.

"Yeah, too bad it's completely wrong," I said.

"What!?" She choked on a piece of onion, and drank down half of her iced tea before resurfacing.

"I said: he got it all wrong."

"What do you mean?"

"Well, for one thing, Brody didn't kill Lissa Boaz. He was there during the evening, to be sure, but in his state of physical and mental deterioration, he couldn't have hurt anyone, save by accident."

"Uh, well, then, uh, who did?" she asked.

"Either Gully or you," I said. "Gully's got the stronger physique, so I suspect it was her. But you could have done it as well: you were there, after all, and if she did it, I suspect you cleaned up the scene afterwards."

"But...but...why would I do such a thing?"

"Because *you* wrote that godawful novel, and there was something—perhaps several somethings—that you didn't want connected to you, or to the person to whom the book was inscribed," I said.

"But you heard Lissa read the inscription out loud," she said.

"I heard what she said—directly to you, by the way—but that wasn't the *real* inscription—which was, in fact, on the title page, as you well knew, having penned it yourself. No, the real inscription was written to your daughter, Gully, when she was an infant, so she'd know who her mother—and by inference, her father—was. Unfortunately, that father was also *your* father, and that was the secret that you couldn't let become public knowledge."

"But what about Brody?"

"*You* killed him, because he knew too much, and he was a danger to Gully. He'd gotten in over his head with his drinking and gambling and ill-temper, and you were afraid that in the end, he would harm her, physically or mentally. So, you arranged something on the stairwell. I don't know what it was, and the police didn't find it in any case—and Gully had no suspicions, so you were safe there. Does she know that you're her mother, by the way?"

I heard Margie sob just once, under her breath, just a little catch in her chest, and then she straightened herself up and looked me in the eye. "Yes, she knows— but not for long. I told her last year. We're working things out as we go."

"Well, you're both free and clear, and I'll try to make sure it stays that way."

"What about Freddie the Cur? I didn't have anything to do with that, and I was afraid…."

"No, Gully didn't kill him, although he certainly had it coming. But, he would have used the knowledge that he'd gained from *Castle Dred* either to blackmail one or the both of you—or worse, to do what Lissa intended to do, which was sell it to the highest bidder, and damn the consequences. They were two of a kind."

"So, who killed him?" she asked.

"Why, *I did*, of course," I said, "and I don't regret it one whit. You're my partner, after all, and you rescued me from myself many years ago, so I owe you big-time for that—and for many, many subsequent years of friendship and good humor.

"Like I said once, we might as well be an old married couple, because we've sorta evolved that way over the decades. I did what I had to do to protect you—and I'd do it again.

"You suffered through terrible circumstances as a young woman. I can't imagine living through what you faced, and then having to give up your child to adoption on top of that. But, you survived, and she survived, and now you've had to relive it all over again. We'll get through this somehow."

She shook her head sadly. "I can never look at things the same way again. I killed a man. I had to do it for my daughter's sake, to protect her—and she killed someone too. And so did you. We're a fine bunch,

aren't we?'"

"Hey, just a typical American family," I said. "Families who slay together play together!—or some such thing. I certainly regret taking a life, *any* life, but Freddie was a particularly nasty individual, and there was no justice under the law that would have suited the circumstances. Having that information made public would have destroyed two worthy lives.

"In any case, what's done is done. The police seem satisfied with the answers they've got, and I suspect that Freddie's killer will never be caught. But if he is, he's lived a good long life, and he'll leave it with no regrets."

She nodded her head slightly. "Very well. We won't talk about this ever again, right?"

"Right," I agreed.

"By the way, what happened to the book?"

"Oh, I almost forgot." I reached into my coat pocket and pulled out *The Secret of Castle Dred.* "A small gift from someone who cares. If it were mine, I'd burn the damned thing. It wasn't your best work anyway, believe me!"

"We all have to start somewhere," she said, taking it from my hands, and putting it away in her purse.

And then, amidst the chorus of olés sprinkling down from the tube above us, we went back to munching on our munchies, which was, after all, the best thing we'd done all day.

AFTERWORD
"CHEAP THRILLS AND CHILLS"

In October of 1964, at the age of sixteen, I went to work in my Dad's service station in Spokane, Washington, and for the first time in my life, I had some real pocket money. I'd long been dissatisfied with the selection of fiction at the local public library, so I immediately began haunting two downtown bookstores: Clark's Old Book Store (run by Jerome "Jerry" Peltier), and Dean Gilbert's Inland Book Store. Both included a healthy selection of used science fiction paperbacks for cheap prices, and so I started visiting them on a weekly basis, quickly building a collection (I never threw anything away). I would sometimes spend every penny that I had on books, and then be forced to hike the seven miles home, instead of taking the bus. I still regret the few titles that "got away."

I also purchased some pbs from the local newstands, but these were much more expensive, costing 40-50 cents each, which I thought exorbitant at the time.

From the very start, I loved mass market paperbacks: the cheap paper, the garish cover art, the sometimes wild writing—all of these things thrilled me

then, and continue to thrill me now. I've always had the collecting instinct, and I began filling in my back-lists of SF, fantasy, and horror paperbacks, whenever I could. I attended my first SF convention in 1968, which led almost immediately to my first book, *Stella Nova*. My life since then has reflected an abiding interest in literature in all its forms. And although I've been quasi-literate since the age of four, my *real* love of books began with the creation of my own library of paperbound fiction—and I've never stopped since.

So, this little mystery, *The Paperback Show Murders*, is my homage to a field that helped make me what I am today—as writer and editor and man. This is my eleventh novel, so you'd think I'd know better by now—but I couldn't resist adding a few funnies to the text. The old pb publishers did indeed issue some true classics of popular literature that deserve to be resurrected and reread. But these were interspersed with some truly dreadful (and now unreadable) novels by hack writers, a fact that often seems to be overlooked by historians of the field. For every title worth reprinting, there are twenty or more that ought to be buried in as deep as hole as one can find—and sealed solidly with lead!

So, I hope you enjoy this excursion into the collecting world. I certainly had a great deal of fun writing it!

—Robert Reginald
San Bernardino, California
20 February 2011

ABOUT THE AUTHOR

ROBERT REGINALD was born in Japan, and lived in Turkey as a youth. He starting writing as a child, and penned his first book during his senior year in college. He settled in Southern California in 1969, where he served as an academic librarian for forty years. He currently edits the Borgo Press Imprint of Wildside Press, and has also penned more than 120 books and 13,000 short pieces. His recent works of fiction include: four Nova Europa historical fantasies, *The Dark-Haired Man; or, The Hieromonk's Tale* (2004), *The Exiled Prince; or, The Archquisitor's Tale* (2004), *Quæstiones; or, The Protopresbyter's Tale* (2005), and *The Fourth Elephant's Egg; or, The Hypatomancer's Tale* (forthcoming); four science fiction novels, *Invasion!: Earth vs. the Aliens* (2007; a trilogy comprising *Invasion!, Operation: Crimson Storm,* and *The Martians Strike Back!*), *Knack' Attack: A Tale of the Human-Knacker War* (2010), *"A Glorious Death": A Tale of the Human-Knacker War* (forthcoming), and *Academentia: A Future Dystopia* (forthcoming); two Phantom Detective period mysteries, *The Phantom's Phantom* (2007) and *The Nasty Gnomes* (2008); a comic mystery, *The Paperback Show Murders* (2011); and three story collections, *Katydid & Other Critters: Tales of Fantasy and Mystery* (2001), *The Elder of Days: Tales of the Elders* (2010), and *The Judgment of the Gods and Other Verdicts of History* (2011). You can find him at:

www.millefleurs.tv